Learn Czech with Beginner Stories

HypLern Interlinear Project
www.hyplern.com

First edition: 2025, November

Author: Karel Jaromír Erben
Translation: Kees van den End
Foreword: Camilo Andrés Bonilla Carvajal PhD

ISBN: 978-1-83425-108-0

kees@hyplern.com
www.hyplern.com

Learn Czech with Beginner Stories

Interlinear Czech to English

Author
Karel Jaromír Erben

Translation
Kees van den End

HypLern Interlinear Project
www.hyplern.com

The HypLern Method

Learning a foreign language should not mean leafing through page after page in a bilingual dictionary until one's fingertips begin to hurt. Quite the contrary, through everyday language use, friendly reading, and direct exposure to the language we can get well on our way towards mastery of the vocabulary and grammar needed to read native texts. In this manner, learners can be successful in the foreign language without too much study of grammar paradigms or rules. Indeed, Seneca expresses in his sixth epistle that "Longum iter est per praecepta, breve et efficax per exempla[1]."

The HypLern series constitutes an effort to provide a highly effective tool for experiential foreign language learning. Those who are genuinely interested in utilizing original literary works to learn a foreign language do not have to use conventional graded texts or adapted versions for novice readers. The former only distort the actual essence of literary works, while the latter are highly reduced in vocabulary and relevant content. This collection aims to bring the lively experience of reading stories as directly told by their very authors to foreign language learners.

Most excited adult language learners will at some point seek their teachers' guidance on the process of learning to read in the foreign language rather than seeking out external opinions. However, both teachers and learners lack a general reading technique or strategy. Oftentimes, students undertake the reading task equipped with nothing more than a bilingual dictionary, a grammar book, and lots of courage. These efforts often end in frustration as the student builds mis-constructed nonsensical sentences after many hours spent on an aimless translation drill.

Consequently, we have decided to develop this series of interlinear translations intended to afford a comprehensive edition of unabridged texts. These texts are presented as they were originally written with no changes in word choice or order. As a result, we have a translated piece conveying the true meaning under every word from the original work. Our readers receive then two books in just one volume: the original version and its translation.

The reading task is no longer a laborious exercise of patiently decoding unclear and seemingly complex paragraphs. What's more, reading becomes an enjoyable and meaningful process of cultural, philosophical and linguistic learning. Independent learners can then acquire expressions and vocabulary while understanding pragmatic and socio-cultural dimensions of the target language by reading in it rather than reading about it.

Our proposal, however, does not claim to be a novelty. Interlinear translation is as old as the Spanish tongue, e.g. "glosses of [Saint] Emilianus", interlinear bibles in Old German, and of course James Hamilton's work in the 1800s. About the latter, we remind the readers, that as a revolutionary freethinker he promoted the publication of Greco-Roman classic works and further pieces in diverse languages. His effort, such as ours, sought to lighten the exhausting task of looking words up in large glossaries as an educational practice: "if there is any thing which fills reflecting men with melancholy and regret, it is the waste of mortal time, parental money, and puerile happiness, in the present method of pursuing Latin and Greek[2]".

Additionally, another influential figure in the same line of thought as Hamilton was John Locke. Locke was also the philosopher and translator of the Fabulae AEsopi in an interlinear plan. In 1600, he was already suggesting that interlinear texts, everyday communication, and use of the target language could be the most appropriate ways to achieve language learning:

> ...the true and genuine Way, and that which I would propose, not only as the easiest and best, wherein a Child might, without pains or Chiding, get a Language which others are wont to be whipt for at School six or seven Years together...[3]

---

1 "The journey is long through precepts, but brief and effective through examples". Seneca, Lucius Annaeus. (1961) Ad Lucilium Epistulae Morales, vol. I. London: W. Heinemann.

2 In: Hamilton, James (1829?) History, principles, practice and results of the Hamiltonian system, with answers to the Edinburgh and Westminster reviews; A lecture delivered at Liverpool; and instructions for the use of the books published on the system. Londres: W. Aylott and Co., 8, Pater Noster Row. p. 29.

3 In: Locke, John. (1693) Some thoughts concerning education. Londres: A. and J. Churchill. pp. 196-7.

Who can benefit from this edition?

We identify three kinds of readers, namely, those who take this work as a search tool, those who want to learn a language by reading authentic materials, and those attempting to read writers in their original language. The HypLern collection constitutes a very effective instrument for all of them.

1. For the first target audience, this edition represents a search tool to connect their mother tongue with that of the writer's. Therefore, they have the opportunity to read over an original literary work in an enriching and certain manner.
2. For the second group, reading every word or idiomatic expression in its actual context of use will yield a strong association between the form, the collocation, and the context. This will have a direct impact on long term learning of passive vocabulary, gradually building genuine reading ability in the original language. This book is an ideal companion not only to independent learners but also to those who take lessons with a teacher. At the same time, the continuous feeling of achievement produced during the process of reading original authors both stimulates and empowers the learner to study[1].
3. Finally, the third kind of reader will notice the same benefits as the previous ones. The proximity of a word and its translation in our interlinear texts is a step further from other collections, such as the Loeb Classical Library. Although their works might be considered the most famous in this genre, the presentation of texts on opposite pages hinders the immediate link between words and their semantic equivalence in our native tongue (or one we have a strong mastery of).

---

1 Some further ways of using the present work include:

1. As you progress through the stories, focus less on the lower line (the English translation). Instead, try to read through the upper line, staying in the foreign language as long as possible.
2. Even if you find glosses or explanatory footnotes about the mechanics of the language, you should make your own hypotheses on word formation and syntactical functions in a sentence. Feel confident about inferring your own language rules and test them progressively. You can also take notes concerning those idiomatic expressions or special language usage that calls your attention for later study.
3. As soon as you finish each text, check the reading in the original version (with no interlinear or parallel translation). This will fulfil the main goal of this

collection: bridging the gap between readers and original literary works, training them to read directly and independently.

Why interlinear?

Conventionally speaking, tiresome reading in tricky and exhausting circumstances has been the common definition of learning by texts. This collection offers a friendly reading format where the language is not a stumbling block anymore. Contrastively, our collection presents a language as a vehicle through which readers can attain and understand their authors' written ideas.

While learning to read, most people are urged to use the dictionary and distinguish words from multiple entries. We help readers skip this step by providing the proper translation based on the surrounding context. In so doing, readers have the chance to invest energy and time in understanding the text and learning vocabulary; they read quickly and easily like a skilled horseman cantering through a book.

Thereby we stress the fact that our proposal is not new at all. Others have tried the same before, coming up with evident and substantial outcomes. Certainly, we are not pioneers in designing interlinear texts. Nonetheless, we are nowadays the only, and doubtless, the best, in providing you with interlinear foreign language texts.

Handling instructions

Using this book is very easy. Each text should be read at least three times in order to explore the whole potential of the method. The first phase is devoted to comparing words in the foreign language to those in the mother tongue. This is to say, the upper line is contrasted to the lower line as the following example shows:

„Já	vyhrál!“	zvolal	člověk	a	ukázal	na	své	suché
I	won	exclaimed	man	and	(he) showed	at	his	dry
nohy.								
feet								

The second phase of reading focuses on capturing the meaning and sense of the original text. As readers gain practice with the method, they should be able to focus on the target language without getting distracted by the translation. New users of the method, however, may find it helpful to cover the translated lines with a piece of paper as illustrated in the image below. Subsequently, they try to understand the meaning of every word, phrase, and entire sentences in the target language itself, drawing on the translation only when necessary. In this phase, the reader should resist the temptation to look at the translation for every word. In doing so, they will find that they are able to understand a good portion of the text by reading directly in the target language, without the crutch of the translation. This is the skill we are looking to train: the ability to read and understand native materials and enjoy them as native speakers do, that being, directly in the original language.

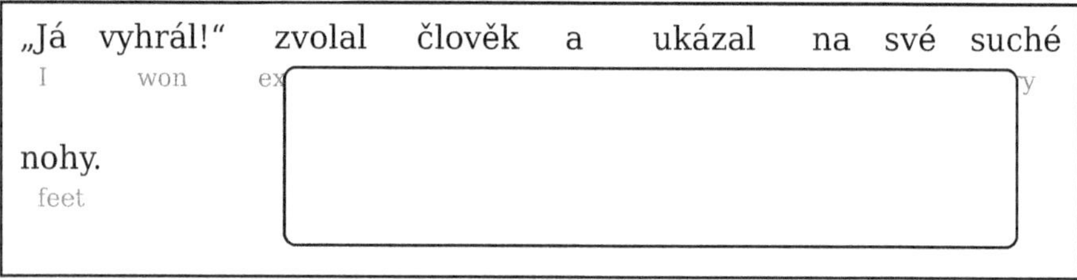
„Já vyhrál!“ zvolal člověk a ukázal na své suché
I won ex y
nohy.
feet

In the final phase, readers will be able to understand the meaning of the text when reading it without additional help. There may be some less common words and phrases which have not cemented themselves yet in the reader's brain, but the majority of the story should not pose any problems. If desired, the reader can use an SRS or some other memorization method to learning these straggling words.

„Já vyhrál!“ zvolal člověk a ukázal na své suché nohy.

Above all, readers will not have to look every word up in a dictionary to read a text in the foreign language. This otherwise wasted time will be spent concentrating on their principal interest. These new readers will tackle authentic texts while learning their vocabulary and expressions to use in further communicative (written or oral) situations. This book is just one work from an overall series with the same purpose. It really helps those who are afraid of having "poor vocabulary" to feel confident about reading directly in the language. To all of them and to all of you, welcome to the amazing experience of living a foreign language!

Additional tools

Check out shop.hyplern.com or contact us at info@hyplern.com for free mp3s (if available) and free empty (untranslated) versions of the eBooks that we have on offer.

For some of the older eBooks and paperbacks we have Windows, iOS and Android apps available that, next to the interlinear format, allow for a pop-up format, where hovering over a word or clicking on it gives you its meaning. The apps also have any mp3s, if available, and integrated vocabulary practice.

Visit the site hyplern.com for the same functionality online. This is where we will be working non-stop to make all our material available in multiple formats, including audio where available, and vocabulary practice.

Table of Contents

Hadí koruna

(The) Snake's Crown

Kdysi	dávno	byla	jedna	maminka,	která
Once upon a time	long ago	(there) was	one	mom	who

měla	malou	dcerku.	Každé	ráno	dostávala
had	(a) little	daughter	Each	morning	received

dcerka	k	snídani	misku	mléka.	Když	jedla,
(the) daughter	for	breakfast	(a) bowl	(of) milk	When	(she) ate

pokaždé	k	ní	přišel	had	a	jedli	spolu.
every time	to	her	came	(a) snake	and	(they) ate	together

Když	oba	dojedli,	šla	dcerka	za	maminkou	a
When	both	finished	went	(the) daughter	to	(the) mom	and

říkala:	„Maminko,	dej	mi	ještě	mléko,	had
(she) said	Mommy	give	me	still	milk	(the) snake

mi	ho	snědl.“
(of) me	it	ate

Maminka	nevěděla,	co	tím	myslí,	ale	vždycky	jí
Mom	didn't know	what	of it	to think	but	always	her

ještě mléko přidala. Takto se to dělo celých
still milk added by Like so itself went this thing (a) whole

sedm let.
seven years

Sedmý rok had řekl dcerce: „Pojď
(In the) seventh year (the) snake said (to the) daughter Go

se mnou. Kudy projdu já, projdeš též. Až
with me Where will go I (you) go also When

dojdeme ke mně domů, řekni, že chceš
we'll get there to my home say that (you) want

korunu. Nabídnou ti něco jiného, ale ty
(the) crown (They) will offer you something else but you

si vezmi jedině tu korunu. Jakmile ji získáš,
yourself take only that crown As soon as her (you) get

splní ti, cokoliv si budeš přát."
(it) will fulfill you anything yourself (you) will wish

Dcerka šla s hadem do jeho domu. Starý
(The) daughter went with (the) snake to its home (The) old

had se podíval a ptal se: „Kdo to je?“
snake itself looked and asked itself Who this is

Mladý had odpověděl: „To je ta dcerka, co mi
(The) young snake answered This is this daughter who me

dává mléko. Něco by chtěla.“
gives milk Something would (she) wanted

Starý had se zeptal: „A co by chtěla?“
(The) old snake itself asked And what would (she have) wanted

Dcerka odpověděla: „Ráda bych dostala
(The) daughter answered Gladly (I) would got
I would like to get

korunu.“
(the) crown

Starý had řekl: „Dám ti něco jiného,
(The) old snake said (I) will give you something else

korunu nechtčj.“
(the) crown (you) don't want

Dcerka si ale přišla pro korunu.
(The) daughter herself however came for (the) crown
went

Nakonec jí starý had korunu dal a
Finally her (the) old snake (the) crown gave and

dcerka se vrátila domů.
(the) daughter herself returned home

Když přišla domů, dala korunu do skříně
When (she) came home (she) put (the) crown onto (a) cabinet

a přála si: „Kéž bych měla skříň plnou
and wished herself If only (I) would (have) had (a) cabinet full

peněz!“
(of) money

A skříň se naplnila až k prasknutí
And (the) cabinet itself filled then to burst(ing)

penězi.
(with) money

Potom dala korunu mezi šaty a přála
Then (she) put (the) crown between (the) dresses and wished

si: „Kéž bych měla hodně krásných šatů!“
herself If only (I) would (have) had a lot (of) beautiful dresses

5

A skříň se zaplnila šaty.
And (the) cabinet itself filled (with) dresses

Potom dala korunu mezi obilí a přála
Then (she) put (the) crown between (the) grain and wished

si: „Kéž bych měla hodně obilí!“
herself If only (I) would (have) had a lot (of) grain

A stalo se. Najednou se objevily kupy
And (it) happened itself At once itself appeared piles

obilí.
(of) grain

Nabrala si trochu obilí a s korunou vše
(She) retrieved herself a little grain and with (the) crown all

poslala do mlýna. Ale v mlýně už korunu
sent to (the) mill But in (the) mill already (the) crown

nikdy neviděla. Mlynář ji taky neviděl. Koruna
never not saw (The) miller her also not saw (The) crown

totiž spadla do vody u mlýna a odnesla ji
namely dropped into (the) water at (the) mill and took her

řeka.

(the) river

Hodné děti

(The) Good Children

Lidé	zapomněli	na	Matku	Bohyni	a
(The) people	forgot	about	(the) Mother	Goddess	and

přestali	ji	uctívat.	Místo	ní	začali
(they) stopped	her	to worship	(In) place	(of) her	(they) started

uctívat	Slunce	jako	boha	oblohy.
(to) worship	(the) Sun	as	god	of the sky

V	té	době	přišlo	na	zemi	velké	sucho,	které
In	that	time	arrived	in	(the) country	(a) great	draught	which

trvalo	několik	let	po	sobě.	Když	lidé	zaseli,
endured	several	years	after	each other	When	people	sowed,

nic	z	toho	nevyrostlo,	nebyla	žádná
nothing	from	this	did not grow	(there) was not	any

úroda.
harvest

Lidi ohrožoval veliký hlad, umírali a
People threatened great hunger (they) were dying and

zvířata hynula hladem. Slunce nepřestávalo
animals perished (from) hunger (The) sun did not stop

pálit a spálilo všechno, co rostlo.
to burn and burned all what grew

V té době vládl mladý car. A jak to bývá,
In that time ruled (a) young tsar And like this is habit

mladí lidé mají rádi mladé, i car měl
young people have gladly young and (the) tsar had
rather other young people

kolem ve svém okruhu jen mladé lidi. V
around in his entourage only young people In

radě, v úřadech i ve vojsku měl jen
(the) council in (the) offices and in (the) military (he) had only

mladé, nezkušené lidi, a tak byly i jejich
young inexperienced people and yes were also their

rady špatné.
counsels wrong

Když	viděli	všude	kolem	bídu,	poradili
When	(they) saw	everywhere	around	misery	(they) advised

carovi,	aby	nechal	všechny	staré	lidi	utopit.
(to the) tsar	to	let	all	old	people	drown

Prý	proto,	že	starci	jedí	chleba	mladým
Reportedly	therefore	that	old people	eat	bread	(of the) young

a	nijak	jim	nepřispívají.	Car	tedy	po
and	nothing	to them they	do not contribute	(The) tsar	so	after

jejich	radě	přikázal,	že	každý,	kdo	se
their	counsel	ordered	that	each	who	themselves

jen	pokusí	ochránit	starého	člověka,	bude
only (even)	will try	to protect	(an) old	person	will be

potrestán	smrtí.
punished	(with) death

Vojáci	se	rozběhli	po	zemi	a
Soldiers	themselves	started running	through	(the) country	and

všude,	kde	našli	starého	člověka,	bez
everywhere	where	(they) found	(an) old	person	without

milosti ho utopili.
mercy him drowned

Ve městě však žili tři bratři, kteří měli
In (the) city however lived three brothers who had

starého otce. Místo aby ho dali vojákům,
(an) old father Place to him (they) gave (to the) soldiers
Instead that

schovali ho doma ve sklepě. Stařeček tam
(they) hid him (at) home in (the) cellar (The) old man there

zůstal několik měsíců a synové mu nosili jídlo.
stayed several months and (the) sons him carried food

Přišlo jaro a nastal čas sázet obilí, ale
Arrived spring and occurred time to plant (the) grain but

nikde nebylo ani zrnko. Všechno se snědlo nebo
nowhere not was any grain All itself ate or

zkazilo.
spoiled

Bratři šli tedy za otcem a ptali se,
Brothers (they) went so to (the) father and asked themselves

co mají dělat. Otec jim poradil: „Sundejte
what (they) have to do (The) father them advised Take down

starou střechu z domu, vymlaťte došky a
(the) old roof from (the) home beat (the) thatch and

zrní z došků zasejte.“
grain from (the) thatch sow

Synové to udělali a Matka Bohyně jim
(The) sons this did and (the) Mother Goddess them

požehnala: za týden se na poli objevilo
blessed after (a) week itself on (the) field appeared

mladé obilí, zelené jako tráva, a za dva
(the) young grain green as grass and after two

měsíce rostly na poli vysoké klasy. Vyrostlo
months grew on (the) field high ears of grain Grew up

žito, pšenice, ječmen a další obilí.
(the) rye wheat barley and next (the) grain

Všichni lidé se nad tím podivovali a
All people themselves over that wondered and

zpráva	se	donesla	až	k	carovi.	Car
(a) message	itself	(was) brought	then	to	(the) tsar	(The) tsar

přikázal,	aby	se	k	němu	bratři
ordered	in order that	itself	to	him	(the) brothers

dostavili.
delivered were brought

Bratři	se	báli	a	šli	znovu	za
(The) brothers	themselves were	feared afraid	and	(they) went	again	for

otcem	pro	radu.	Otec	jim	řekl:	„Jen	jděte	a
(the) father	for	advice	Father	them	said	Just	go	and

řekněte	carovi	pravdu."
tell	(the) tsar	(the) truth

Bratři	tedy	šli	k	carovi	a	ten	se	na
(The) brothers	so	went	to	(the) tsar	and	this one	himself	at

ně	rozhněval.	Zeptal	se,	proč	schovávají
them	angered	Asked	himself	why	hide

obilí,	když	v	jejich	carství	panuje	tak	hrozivý
(the) grain	when	in	their	tsardom kingdom	prevails	such	terrifying

hlad a umírají lidé. Bratři mu všechno
hunger and die people (The) brothers him all

pravdivě vysvětlili, přesně jak se to stalo, od
truthfully explained exactly how itself this happened from

začátku až do konce. Poté řekli: „A teď,
(the) start until to (the) end Then (they) said And now

nejmilostivější care, udělej s námi, co
most gracious tsar do with us what

uznáš za vhodné.“
(you) recognize for appropriate

Car se ale uklidnil a nakonec
(The) tsar himself however calmed down and finally

přikázal, aby mu přivedli jejich otce.
ordered in order that him (they) brought their father

Car otce posadil vedle sebe a poslouchal
(The) tsar (the) father sat next to himself and listened to

jeho rady až do své smrti. Bratry za jejich
his advice until to his death (The) brothers for their

dobré	srdce	bohatě	odměnil.
good	heart	richly	(he) rewarded

Pohádka o Jednooké bídě

(The) Tale of One-Eyed Misery

Žil	kdysi	jeden	kovář.	Říkal	si:
Lived	once upon a time	one	blacksmith	(He) told	himself

„Nikdy	jsem	neviděl	Bídu.	Říkají,	že	je	na
Never	(I) am	not saw	Misery	(They) say	that	is	on
	I have	seen					

světě	Bída,	tak	ji	půjdu	najít."	Napil	se,
(the) world	Misery	yes	her	(I) will go	find	(He) drank	himself
						He drank	

oblékl	a	vydal	se	hledat	Bídu.
dressed	and	gave out	himself	to search	Misery
		set out			

Po	cestě	potkal	krejčího.	„Pozdrav	Pán	Bůh!"
On	(the) road	(he) met	(a) tailor	Get well	lord	god
				May bless you		

– „Pán	Bůh	s	vámi!"
– Lord	god	with	you

– „Kam	to	jdete?"
– Where	this	(you) go to
		(formal)

– „Hledám Bídu, říkají, že se potuluje světem,
– Looking for Misery (they) say who itself roams (the) world

ale já ji nikdy neviděl."
but I her never not saw

– „Tak pojď, půjdeme spolu. Mně se taky dobře
– Yes go (we)'ll go together To me itself also well

vede, Bídu neznám."
leads Misery (I) don't know
comes out

Šli spolu, až došli do hustého,
(They) went together then (they) reached to (a) dense

temného lesa. Narazili tam na malou
dark forest (They) came across there on (a) small

cestičku. Šli po ní, až došli k
path (They) went on (of) her then (they) reached to

velkému stavení. Byla noc a neměli kde
(a) great building (It) was night and (they) not had (any)where

spát, proto souhlasně řekli: „Půjdeme tam."
(to) sleep therefore agreed (they) said (We)'ll go there
they said in agreement

Vešli dovnitř, ale nikoho tam nenašli. Bylo
(They) went inside but no-one there not found (It) was

tam prázdno a přišlo jim to jako strašidelné
there empty and arrived to them this as (a) scary
seemed

místo. Sedli si a čekali.
place (They) seated themselves and waited

Najednou přišla vysoká, hubená žena, která měla
At once (she) came (a) tall skinny woman who had

jen jedno oko. „Aha!“ řekla, „nečekala jsem hosty.
only one eye Aha (she) said not expected (I) am guests
I have

Vítám vás!“
Welcome to you

– „Děkujeme, babičko, přišli jsme k vám domů
– Thank you grandma came (we) are to your home

strávit noc.“
to spend (the) night

– „Dobře, budu mít co večeřet!“
– Good (then I) will have something to dine (on)

Ti dva se polekali. Žena šla,
Those two themselves scared (The) woman went
got scared

přinesla dříví, hodila ho do pece a
brought along firewood tossed it into (the) furnace and

zapálila oheň. Potom vzala krejčího, zařízla ho
lit (a) fire Then (she) took (the) tailor cut up him

a hodila do pece. Kovář seděl a
and tossed into (the) furnace (The) blacksmith sat and

přemýšlel, co dělat.
thought what to do

Žena vytáhla upečené maso a začala večeřet.
(The) woman pulled up (the) baked meat and started to dine
to eat

Kovář jí řekl: „Babičko, já jsem kovář."
(The) blacksmith her said Grandma I am (a) blacksmith

– „Co umíš?"
– What can (you) do

– „Umím kovat."
– (I) can forge

– „Tak mi ukovej oko.“
– Yes me forge (an) eye

– „Dobře,“ řekl kovář, „ale musíš se
– Good said (the) blacksmith but must yourself

nechat svázat, jinak to nepůjde.“
let tie otherwise this won't work

Žena souhlasila a přinesla dva provazy, tenký
(The) woman agreed and brought two ropes thin

a pevný. Kovář ji svázal tenkým
and firm (The) blacksmith her bound (with the) thin

provazem, ale žena ho lehce přetrhla.
rope but (the) woman him easily she broke

„To nejde, babičko,“ řekl. Potom ji svázal
This not goes grandma (he) said Then her (he) bound
doesn't work

pevným provazcm. „Teď se převal!“ Žena
(with) firm rope Now yourself roll over (The) woman

se převalila, ale už provaz nepřetrhla.
herself rolled over but already (the) rope did not break

Kovář vzal rozžhavené železo a přiložil jí
(The) Blacksmith took (a) hot iron and stuck her

ho na zdravé oko. Pak vzal sekyru a udeřil
it in (the) healthy eye Then (he) took (an) axe and (he) hit

na železo. Žena se převalila, přetrhla
on (the) iron (The) woman herself rolled over broke

provaz a sedla si na práh. „Ha,
(the) rope and seated herself on (the) threshold Ha

padouchu, teď mi neutečeš!“ Kovář viděl,
villain now me (you) can't escape (The) blacksmith saw

že je v nebezpečí, a přemýšlel, co dělat.
that (he) is in danger and thought what to do

Večer se vracely ovečky a žena
(In the) evening themselves returned (the) sheep and (the) woman

je zahnala do domu. Kovář zůstal přes noc
is drove to home (The) blacksmith stayed over- night
them drove home

u ní v domě. Ráno žena začala
at her in (the) home (In the) morning (the) woman started

ovce pouštět ven. Kovář si na sebe
(the) sheep to let out (The) blacksmith himself on himself

vzal ovčí kožich, otočil ho srstí nahoru a
took (a) sheep skin turned it fur up and

připlížil se k ženě po čtyřech jako ovce.
sneaked himself to (the) woman on (all) four(s) like (a) sheep

Žena vždycky ovci popadla a vyhodila ven.
(The) woman always (a) sheep grabbed and threw out

Kovář tedy přilezl v kožichu, a žena
(the) blacksmith so (he) came in skin and (the) woman

ho popadla a vyhodila. Jakmile byl venku,
him grabbed and threw out As soon as (he) was outside

vstal a řekl: „Sbohem, Bído! Už mi
(he) stood up and said Goodbye Misery Already me

nemůžeš nic udělat.“ Ale Bída odpověděla:
(you) can't nothing do But Misery answered

„Počkej, ještě uvidíš!“
Wait still (you) will see

Kovář šel dál lesem a našel
(The) blacksmith went to continue (through the) woods and found

ve stromě sekyrku se zlatou rukojetí. Chtěl
in (a) tree (an) ax with (a) golden handle (He) wanted

si ji vzít, ale jakmile ji chytil, přilepila mu
himself her take but as soon as her grabbed stuck him

ruka a nemohl se od sekery odtrhnout.
(the) hand and (he) couldn't itself from (the) ax tear off

Ohlédl se a viděl, jak se k němu
(He) looked back himself and saw how itself to him

přibližuje Bída. „Neutečeš mi," volala.
approached Misery (You) can't escape me (she) called

Kovář vytáhl nůž a odřízl si ruku,
(The) blacksmith got out (a) knife and cut off himself (the) hand

aby utekl.
in order that (he) escaped

Vrátil se do své vesnice a ukazoval lidem,
Returned himself to his village and showed people
explained

jak	přišel	o	ruku.	Říkal:	„Teď	už	vím,
how	came he lost	about	(the) hand	He said	Now	already	(I) know

jak	vypadá	Bída.	Sežrala	mého	kamaráda	a
how	looks	Misery	(She) devoured	my	friend	and

mně	vzala	ruku.“
from me	took	(the) hand

Lipka

Lime

Jednoho večera seděl Vaňuša se svým dědečkem
One dinner seated Vanusha himself to his grandpa

a zeptal se ho: „Dědečku, proč mají medvědi
and asked from him Grandpa why have bears

tlapy tak podobné našim rukám a nohám?“
paws so similar to our hands and feet

Dědeček odpověděl: „Poslouchej, Vaňušo! Co jsem
Grandfather answered Listen Vanusha What (I) am
I have

slyšel od starších lidí, to ti povím. Starší lidé
heard from elder people this you I'll tell Older people

říkali, že medvědi bývali lidé jako my,
said that bears used to be people like us

křesťané.“
christians

V jedné vesnici žil chalupník. Měl starý dům,
In one village lived (a) cottager (He) had (an) old house

neměl koně ani krávu, a dříví také neměl.
didn't have horses nor (a) cow and firewood also didn't

Když přišla zima, bylo v chalupě chladno.
When came winter (it) was in (the) cottage cold

Chalupník vzal sekyru a šel do lesa. Tam
(The) cottager took (an) axe and went to (the) forest There

našel kouzelný strom – lipku.
(he) found (a) magical tree – (a) lime

Udeřil do ní sekyrou a strom promluvil
(He) hit on her (with his) axe and (the) tree spoke

lidským hlasem: „Co vše si budeš přát,
(with a) human voice What all yourself (you) will wish

to ti dám. Pokud nemáš bohatství nebo
this you (I) will give If (you) don't have wealth or

ženu, nevadí, dám ti všechno.“
woman never mind (I) will give you all

Chalupník odpověděl: „Dobře, matičko Lipko.
(The) cottager answered Good mother Lime

Chtěl bych být bohatší než ostatní sedláci. Nemám
Wanted would be richer than other peasants (I) have no
I would like to be

krávu, koně ani pořádný dům.“ Lipka řekla: „Jdi
cow horses nor (a) proper house Lime said Go

domů. Všechno budeš mít!“
home All (you) will have

Chalupník šel domů a tam na něj čekal nový
(The) cottager went home and there for him waited (a) new

dům, koně, co vypadali jako z pohádky,
house horses that looked like (it was) from (a) fairy tale

a stodola plnou obilí. Ale měl nehezkou
and (a) barn full (of) grain But (it) had (an) unseemly

ženu, což mu vadilo. Řekl si: „Půjdu znovu
woman which him bothered (He) told himself (I) will go again

k Lipce.“ Vzal sekyru a šel zpět do
to Lime (He) took (an) axe and went to back to

lesa.
(the) forest

Když přišel k Lipce, udeřil ji sekyrou a ona
When (he) came to Lime (he) hit her (with the) axe and she

se zeptala: „Co chceš?“ – „Matičko Lipko,
herself asked What (do you) want – Mother Lime

ostatní muži mají krásné ženy a já mám takovou
other men have beautiful women and I have such

nehezkou. Můžeš mi dát krásnou ženu?“
(an) unseemly (one) Can me (you) give (a) beautiful woman

Lipka řekla: „Jdi domů.“
Lime said Go home

Chalupník přišel domů a tam ho čekala
(The) cottager came home and there him awaited

krásná žena, jako z pohádky. Žili spolu
(a) beautiful woman like from (a) fairy tale (They) lived together

šťastně, ale chalupník chtěl víc. Pomyslel si:
happily but (the) cottager wanted more Thought himself

„Dobře se nám žije, ale pořád jsme pod
Good ourselves us lives but still (we) are under

správou. Nemohl bych být starostou?“
(someone's) rule (Is it) impossible (that I) would be mayor

Šel opět k Lipce.
(He) went again to Lime

Lipka se ho znovu zeptala: „Co chceš,
Lime herself him again asked What (you) want

sedláku?“ – „Chtěl bych být starostou.“ Lipka
farmer – Wanted (I) would be mayor Lime

odpověděla: „Jdi domů, budeš starosta!“ Když
answered Go home (you) will be mayor When

přišel domů, už na něj čekal dopis, že se
came home already on him waited (a) letter that himself

stal starostou. Žil jako starosta, ale pořád
(he) became mayor (He) lived as mayor but still

nebyl spokojený. Řekl si: „Dobře být
(he) was not satisfied (He) said (to) himself Good to be

starostou, ale nemohl bych být pánem?" Šel
mayor but couldn't (I) would be lord (He) went

opět k Lipce.
again to Lime

Lipka se zeptala: „Co chceš tentokrát?" –
Lime herself asked What (you) want this time –

„Chci být pánem, abych nemusel nikomu
(I) want to be lord so that (I) didn't have to (for) anyone

smekat klobouk." Lipka odpověděla: „Dobře, jdi
take off (the) hat Lime answered Good go

domů." A tak se z chalupníka stal
home And yes itself from (the) cottager became

šlechtic. Začal pořádat oslavy a hostiny. Ale
(a) nobleman Started to host celebrations and banquets But

pořád chtěl víc. Řekl si: „Dobře být
still (he) wanted more (He) said (to) himself Good to be

šlechticem, ale co kdybych byl úředníkem?" Opět
(a) nobleman but what if I was (an) official Again

šel k Lipce.
(he) went to Lime

„Co chceš teď?“ zeptala se Lipka. Chalupník
What (you) want now asked herself Lime (The) cottager

řekl: „Chci být úředníkem.“ Lipka mu opět řekla:
said (I) want to be (an) official Lime him again (she) said

„Jdi domů.“ A opravdu, stal se z něj
Go home And really became itself from him

úředník. Ale i tak chtěl víc. Pomyslel
(an) official But and so (he) wanted more (He) thought

si: „Dobře být úředníkem, ale chtěl bych
(by) himself Good to be (an) official but wanted (I) would

být guvernérem.“ Šel znovu k Lipce.
be (the) governor (He) went again to Lime

Lipka se ho zeptala: „Čeho chceš teď?“
Lime herself him asked Of what (you) want now

Chalupník odpověděl: „Chci být guvernérem.“
(The) cottager answered (I) want to be (the) governor

Lipka řekla: „Dobře, budeš guvernér." A tak

Lime (she) said Good (you) will be governor And yes

se stal guvernérem. Ale i když byl

himself (he) became governor But also when (he) was

guvernér, pořád nebyl spokojený. Chtěl být

governor still (he) was not satisfied (He) wanted be

králem.

king

Šel znovu k Lipce a řekl: „Chci být králem!"

(He) went again to Lime and said (I) want to be king

Lipka ho začala přemlouvat: „Nerozumný člověče,

Lime him started to persuade Unreasonable man

co to žádáš? Už jsi dosáhl všeho, co

what (is) this (you) ask Already (you) are reached all what

jsi chtěl, a král je zvolen Bohem." Lipka ho

(you) are wanted and king is chosen by god Lime him

varovala, že pokud bude dál naléhat, ztratí

assured that if (he) would continue to insist (he) loses

všechno. Chalupník si ale nedal říct a
everything (The) cottager himself however didn't give say and

pořád prosil, aby ho udělala králem.
still asked in order that him (she) made king

Nakonec mu Lipka řekla: „Dobře, když tolik
Finally him Lime (she) said Good when so much

chceš, budeš medvědem a tvoje žena
(you) want (you) will (a) bear and your wife

medvědicí." A tak se z chalupníka stal
(a female) bear And indeed itself from (the) cottager became

medvěd a z jeho ženy medvědice. A
(a) bear and from his woman (a female) bear And

tak vznikli medvědi.
so originated bears
that's where bears came from

Vnouček se zeptal: „Dědečku, je to pravda?"
(The) grandson himself asked Grandpa is this (the) truth

Dědeček odpověděl: „Je to jen pohádka. Když
(The) grandfather answered Is this only (a) fairy tale When
This is

chceš	víc,	než	je	možné,	můžeš	přijít	o
(you) want	more	than	is	possible	(you) can	come lose	about

všechno.	Buď	rád	za	to,	co	máš.“
everything	Be	happy	for	this	what	you have

Sněhurka

Snow-Little (Snow White)

Byl	jednou	sedlák	jménem	Ivan,	který	měl
(There) was	once	(a) farmer	by the name	(of) Ivan	who	had

ženu	Marii.	Byli	už	staří	a	neměli
(a) wife	Marie	(They) were	already	old	and	(they) not had

žádné	děti,	což	je	velmi	trápilo.	Jednou	v
any	children	which	them	much	bothered	Once	in

zimě,	když	napadl	sníh	po	kolena,	viděli	venku
winter	when	fell	snow	up to	(the) knees	(they) saw	outside

děti,	jak	si	staví	sněhuláka.	Ivan	se
children	how	themselves	(they) build	(a) snowfigure a snowman	Ivan	himself

usmál	a	řekl:	„Pojď,	ženo,	postavíme	si
smiled	and	said	(Let's) go	wife	(we) will build	ourselves

taky	sněhuláka.“
also	(a) snowman

Marie se zasmála a odpověděla: „Proč ne? Ale
Marie herself laughed and answered Why not But

místo obyčejného sněhuláka si postavíme
(in) place (of an) ordinary snowman ourselves (we) will build

sněhové děťátko, když nám Bůh nedal
(a) snow baby when us god didn't give

opravdové.“
(a) real one

Ivan souhlasil a oba šli ven. Ze sněhu
Ivan agreed and both (they) went out From snow

začali tvořit děťátko – udělali tělíčko, ruce,
(they) started to create (a) baby (they) made (a) body hands

nohy a nakonec přidělali hlavičku.
feet and finally added (a) little head

„Žehnej vám Pán Bůh,“ pozdravil je
Bless you (the) lord god complimented them

kolemjdoucí. „Děkujeme,“ odpověděl Ivan. „Děláme
(a) bystander Thank you answered Ivan (We) make
We are making

sněhové děťátko," dodala Marie se smíchem.
(a) snow baby added Marie herself laughing

Udělali nos, bradu a oči. Když Ivan udělal i
(They) made (a) nose (a) chin and eyes When Ivan made also

ústa, děťátko najednou začalo dýchat! Otevřelo
(the) mouth (the) baby at once started to breathe (It) opened

své modré oči, hýbalo hlavičkou a třepalo
her blue eyes moved (its) little head and shook

ručičkami a nožičkami jako živé.
(the) little arms and (the) little legs as if alive

„Ivane, podívej! Bůh nám dal děťátko!" vykřikla
Ivan look God us gave (a) baby exclaimed

Marie radostně. Děťátko se vylouplo ze své
Marie joyfully (The) baby itself peeled from its

sněhové skořápky, a najednou na jeho stála
snowy shell and at once on its stood

opravdová holčička. „Ach, moje drahá Sněhurko!"
(a) real little girl Ah my dear Little snow
Snow white

volala Marie a vzala holčičku domů.
called Marie and (she) took (the) little girl home

Sněhurka rychle rostla. Každý den byla
Snow white quickly grew Each day (she) was

o kousek větší. Ivan a Marie měli ze
about (a) piece larger Ivan and Marie had from
a little bit

Sněhurky velkou radost. Chodily k nim domů
Snowflake great joy Walked to her home

dívky ze vsi, hrály si
(the) girls from (the) village played themselves
they played

se Sněhurkou a naučily ji vše, co uměly.
herself Snow white and taught her all what (they) could
with Snow white

Sněhurka brzy vypadala jako třináctiletá dívka.
Snow white soon looked as (a) thirteen years old girl

Byla bílá jako sníh, měla modré oči a dlouhé
(She) was white as snow had blue eyes and long

zrzavé vlasy až po pás. Jen neměla vůbec
ginger hair until on waist Only (she) didn't have at all
her

červená líčka, jako kdyby neměla v těle krev.
red cheeks as if (she) didn't have in body blood

Ale i tak byla krásná, milá a hodná, a
But also yes (she) was beautiful sweet and worthy good and

všichni ji měli rádi.
everyone her had liked gladly

„Podívej, Ivane," říkala Marie, „Bůh nám dopřál
See Ivan said Marie god (to) us granted

radost a dal nám dítě!" A Ivan odpověděl:
joy and gave us (a) child And Ivan answered

„Chvála Bohu, jenže radost netrvá věčně, stejně
Praise to god but joy doesn't last forever as well

tak ani smutek."
so neither grief

Když skončila zima, slunce začalo hřát,
When ended (the) winter (the) sun started (to) warm

tráva se zelenala a ptáci začali znovu
(the) grass itself greened and (the) birds started again

zpívat. Děvčata ze vsi se sešla,
to sing Girls from (the) village each other met

aby si zazpívala, ale Sněhurka byla
in order that themselves (they) sung but Snow white was

smutná.
sad

„Co se děje, mé dítě?“ ptala se Marie.
What itself (is) happening my child asked herself Marie

„Nic mi není, matičko, jsem zdravá,“ odpověděla
Nothing me not mother (I) am healthy answered

Sněhurka.
Snow white

Jakmile sníh roztál a vše začalo kvést,
As soon as (the) snow thawed and everything started to bloom

Sněhurka byla jcště smutnější. Vyhýbala se
Snow white was still sadder Shunned herself

slunci a schovávala se ve stínu. Když
(the) sun and hid herself in (the) shade When

pršelo	nebo	bylo	zataženo,	byla	veselejší.
(it) rained	or	(it) was	cloudy	(she) was	happy

Jednou	přišla	bouřka	s	kroupami,	a	to	byla
Once	came	(a) storm	with	hail	and	this	was

Sněhurka	šťastná	jako	nikdy	předtím.	Když	ale
Snow white	happy	as	never	before	When	however

kroupy	roztály	pod	slunečním	žárem,	plakala,	jako
(the) hail	melted	under	(the) sun's	heat	poster	as

by	sama	chtěla	roztát.
would	herself	(she) wanted	to melt

Pak	přišel	den	svatého	Jana.	Děvčata	ze
Then	came	(the) day	(of) saint	Jana	Girls	from

vsi	šla	do	háje	a	přišla	si	i
(the) village	went	to	(the) groves	and	came	themselves	also

pro	Sněhurku.	„Pusť	ji	s	námi,"	prosila	děvčata.
for	Snow white	Let go	her	with	us	begged	(the) girls

Marie	se	bála	ji	pustit,	ale	nakonec
Marie	herself	was afraid	her	to let go	but	finally

povolila. „Jen na ni dejte pozor," řekla. Děvčata
allowed (it) Only on her put attention (she) said (The) girls
Just take care of her

slíbila, že se o Sněhurku postarají,
promised that themselves on Snow white (they) pay attention

vzala ji za ruku a běžela do háje.
took her by (the) hand and ran to (the) groves

Tam všechny dívky pletly věnečky, zpívaly písně
There all (the) girls knitted wreaths sang songs

a hrály hry. Když slunce zapadlo, děvčata
and played games When (the) sun fell (the) girls
set

udělala hranici z trávy a větviček, zapálila
made (a) boundary from grasses and twigs lit

ji a začala přes oheň skákat. Sněhurka měla
her and started over (the) fire to jump Snow white had

skočit jako poslední.
to jump as last

„Sněhurko, koukej se a skoč za námi," volaly
Snow white look yourself and jump after us called

dívky. Začaly zpívat a skákaly přes oheň.
(the) girls (They) started to sing and jumped over (the) fire

Najednou se ozval za nimi tichý vzdech:
At once herself called out behind them (a) quiet sigh

„Ach!“ Všechny se otočily, ale Sněhurka
Ah All themselves turned but Snow white

už tam nebyla.
already there was not

„Asi se schovala,“ myslela si děvčata
Probably herself (she) hid thought by themselves (the) girls

a začala ji hledat. Volaly ji, ale nemohly
and started her to search (They) called her but (they) couldn't

ji najít. Nakonec si řekly, že se
her find Finally themselves (they) told that herself

vrátila domů. Ale doma také nebyla.
(she) returned home But (at) home also (she) was not

Hledaly ji několik dalších dní, prohledaly
(They) searched her several next days (they) searched

celý	háj,	ale	Sněhurku	nikde	nenašly.
(the) whole	grove	but	Snow white	nowhere	not was found

Kam	se	poděla?	Možná	ji	odneslo	zvíře
Where	herself	(she) went to	Maybe	her	carried away	(an) animal

nebo	velký	pták?	Ne.	Když	Sněhurka	skočila	přes
or	(a) large	bird	No	When	Snow white	jumped	over

oheň,	proměnila	se	v	lehký	obláček	a
(the) fire	(she) turned	herself	in	(a) light	little cloud	and

odletěla	do	nebe.
flew away	to	heaven

Ilja Muromec a Slavík loupežník

Ilya Muromets and (the) Nightingale Robber

V	městě	Murom	žil	sedlák	a	měl	syna
In	(the) city	(of) Mura	lived	(a) farmer	and	had	son

jménem	Ilja	Muromec.	Ilja	nemohl	třicet	let
by the name	(of) Ilya	Muromets	Ilya	couldn't	(for) thirty	years

chodit	a	jen	seděl.	Pak	jednoho	dne	vstal
walk	and	only	sat	Then	one	day	(he) stood up

a	pocítil	velkou	sílu.	Vyrobil	si	bojovou
and	felt	great	power	(He) made	himself	combat

zbroj,	osedlal	koně	a	poprosil	své	rodiče	o
arms	saddled	(a) horse	and	asked	his	parents	for

požehnání,	aby	mohl	odjet	do	města
blessings	in order that	(he) could	depart	to	(the) city

Kyjeva pomodlit se k Bohu a poklonit se
(of) Kyiv (to) pray himself to god and bow himself

knížeti Vladimírovi. Rodiče mu dali své
(to) prince Vladimir (The) parents him (they) gave their

požehnání a Ilja vyjel.
blessings and Ilya went out

Když projížděl tmavým lesem, přepadli ho
When (he) went through (the) dark woods raided him

loupežníci a chtěli mu vzít koně. Ilja však
robbers and wanted him to take (the) horse Ilya however

vystřelil na ně šíp a loupežníci se
fired at them (an) arrow and (the) robbers themselves

mu poddali. Ilja jim odpustil, ale varoval je,
him submitted to Ilya them forgave but warned them

aby to už nikdy nezkoušeli.
in order that it already never (they) tried (again)

Ilja pokračoval dál a dorazil k městu
Ilya continued further and arrived to (the) city

Černihiv, které obléhalo velké vojsko nepřátel.
(of) Tsjornihiv which besieged (a) great army (of) enemies

Ti chtěli město dobýt, zničit chrámy a
They wanted (the) city conquer destroy (the) temples and

zajmout knížete. Ilja se rozhodl bránit víru
capture (the) prince Ilya himself decided to defend (the) faith

křesťanskou a začal bojovat. Pobil nepřátele
christian and started to fight (He) killed (the) enemies

a zajal jejich vůdce, kterého přivedl do
and captured their leader who (he) brought to

města. Obyvatelé Černihivu ho slavně přivítali,
(the) city (The) residents (of) Tsjornihiv him as a hero welcomed

poděkovali mu a propustili ho na další cestu.
thanked him and let go him on further road
travel

Ilja se vydal přímo do Kyjeva, ale cesta,
Ilya himself gave out directly to Kyiv but (the) way
directed

kterou jel, byla nebezpečná. Už třicet let
by which (he) rode was dangerous Already thirty years

ji blokoval Slavík loupežník, který nezabíjel
her blocked (the) Nightingale robber who didn't kill

mečem, ale svým silným pískáním. Když Ilja
(by the) sword but (by) his strong whistling When Ilya

projížděl, Slavík začal pískat. Nejprve na
passed (the) Nightingale started to whistle First at
was going through

vzdálenost dvaceti verst, ale Ilju to nezastrašilo.
(a) distance (of) twenty verst but Ilya this undaunted

Potom Slavík pískal ještě silněji na deset
Then (the) Nightingale whistled still stronger at ten

verst, až Iljův kůň zakopl. Přesto jel Ilja dál,
verst then Ilya's horse tripped Yet rode Ilya further

až přijel k hnízdu Slavíka, které bylo
then (he) arrived to (the) nest (of the) Nightingale which was
the lair

na dvanácti dubech. Slavík chtěl Ilju zabít
on twelve oaks (The) Nightingale wanted Ilya kill

svým hvizdem, ale Ilja vzal svůj luk a vystřelil
(with) his whistle but Ilya took his bow and fired

šíp,	který	zasáhl	Slavíka	do	oka.
(an) arrow	which	hit	(the) Nightingale	to	eye
				in	(his) eye

Slavík	padal	z	hnízda	jako	pytel
(The) Nightingale	fell	from	(the) nest	like	(a) sack
			his lair		

brambor.
(of) potato
of potatoes

Ilja	ho	přivázal	k	třmenu	svého	koně	a	vydal
Ilya	him	tied	to	(the) stirrup	(of) his	horse	and	gave out
								directed

se	do	Kyjeva.	Na	cestě	jel	kolem	domů,
himself	to	Kyiv	On	(the) road	(he) rode	past	(the) house

kde	žily	Slavíkovi	tři	dcery.	Nejmladší	z
where	lived	Nightingale's	three	daughters	(The) youngest	from

nich	zavolala:	„Podívejte,	tatíček	se	vrací	s
them	called	See	daddy	himself	returns	with

kořistí	a	veze	s	sebou	zajatce.“	Ale	starší
prey	and	brings	with	himself	(a) captive	But	(the) older

dcera	plakala:	„To	není	tatíček,	to	je
daughter	cried	This	not is	daddy	this	is

cizí	muž	a	veze	našeho	tatínka.“
(a) foreign	man	and	(he) carries	our	dad
a stranger					

Zavolaly	své	muže,	aby	Ilju	zastavili	a
(They) called	their	men	in order that	Ilya	(they) stopped	and

tatínka	mu	vzali.	Jejich	muži	vyrazili
(their) daddy	(from) him	(they) took	Their	men	went out

proti	Iljovi	s	kopími,	ale	Slavík	je	varoval:
against	Ilya	with	spears	but	(the) Nightingale	is	alert

„Neútočte	na	tak	silného	hrdinu,	pokud	chcete
Don't attack	on	such	strong	heroes	if	(you) want

žít.	Raději	ho	pozvěte	do	mého	domu	na
to live	Preferable (that)	him	(you) invite	to	my	house	for

číši	vína.“
(a) glass	(of) wine

Ilja	přijel	do	domu,	ale	Slavíkova	dcera	na
Ilya	arrived	to	(the) house	but	(the) Nightingale's	daughter	on

něj	chtěla	spustit	železnou	bránu.	Ilja	ji	však
him	wanted	to let go	(the) iron	gateway	Ilya	her	however
		to drop					

spatřil a probodl ji kopím. Potom pokračoval
spotted and pierced her (with a) spear Then (he) continued

dál do Kyjeva, kde se setkal s knížetem
further to Kyiv where himself (he) met with prince

Vladimírem. Kníže se ho zeptal, odkud
Vladimir (The) prince himself him asked from where

je a jakou cestou přijel. Ilja mu vyprávěl
(he) is and from which way (he) arrived Ilya him told

o boji s nepřáteli u Černihivu a o
about (the) fight with (the) enemies at Tsjornihiv and about

tom, jak zajal Slavíka loupežníka.
this how (he) captured (the) Nightingale robber

Kníže tomu ale nevěřil. Teprve když
(The) prince this however disbelieved Only when

ostatní bohatýři, Aleša Popovic a Dobryňa
(the) other heroes Alesha Popovic and Dobryna

Nikitič, potvrdili, že Ilja říká pravdu, kníže mu
Nikitich confirmed what Ilya says (the) truth (the) prince him

uvěřil.
believed

Kníže chtěl slyšet Slavíkův loupežnický
(The) prince wanted to hear (the) Nightingale robber's

hvizd, a tak přikázal, aby Slavík
whistle and so ordered in order that (the) Nightingale

zapískal. Slavík varoval, že by mohl
whistled (The) Nightingale warned that would could

všechny ohlušit, ale kníže trval na svém.
all deafen but (the) prince insisted on his (wish) this

Slavík tedy písknul, až všichni bohatýři
(The) Nightingale so then (he) whistled then every hero

padli k zemi. Ilja to nemohl nevydržet a
fell to (the) ground Ilya this couldn't endure and

zabil Slavíka.
killed (the) Nightingale

Potom Ilja pokračoval ve svých hrdinských činech
Then Ilya continued in his heroic actions

a přidal se k bohatýrům. Jednou se potkal
and added himself to (the) heroes Once himself (he) met

s chudým žebrákem, který mu řekl, že Kyjev
with (with a) poor beggar who him told that Kyiv

ohrožuje nebezpečný bojovník jménem Idolisko.
threatens (a) dangerous warrior (by the) name (of) Idol

Ilja se rozhodl vrátit do Kyjeva. Přestrojený za
Ilya himself decided to return to Kyiv Disguised as

žebráka dorazil na knížecí dvůr, kde uviděl
(a) beggar (he) arrived at (the) princely court where (he) saw

Idoliska. Ten snědl býka a vypil kotel
Idol This one ate (a) bull and drank (a) kettledrum

piva. Ilja se rozhodl s ním bojovat.
(of) beer Ilya himself decided with him to fight

V pravou chvíli se odhalil a jedinou
In (the) right while time himself (he) revealed and (with a) single

ranou Idoliska porazil. Kníže Vladimír Iljovi
wound blow Idol beat defeated Prince Vladimir Ilya

poděkoval a přijal ho mezi nejsilnější hrdiny
thanked and accepted him between (the) strongest heroes

v Kyjevě.
in Kyiv

Kurent a člověk

Kurant and Man

Jednou	se	Kurent	a	člověk	začali	hádat
Once	himself	Kurent (mythical creature)	and	(a) man	started	to guess

o	tom,	kdo	má	na	zemi	vládnout.	Člověk
about	this	who	has	over	(the) country	reign	Man

byl	obrovské	postavy	a	plný	síly.	Kurent	se
was	huge	figure	and	full	forces	Kurent	himself

na	něj	podíval	a	řekl:	„Pojď,	vyzkoušíme,	kdo	z
at	him	looked	and	said	Go	try	who	from

nás	je	silnější.	Kdo	zvítězí,	bude	vládnout	na
us	is	stronger	Who	will win	will	reign	over

zemi.	Vidíš	to	moře?	Pojďme	ho
(the) country	(You) see	this	sea	Let go us	it

přeskočit.	Kdo	skočí	lépe,	ten	vyhraje.“
(we) jump across	Who	jumps	better	this one	will win

Člověk souhlasil, a tak si Kurent pozdvihl
Man agreed and yes himself Kurent raised

halenu a skočil přes celé moře, ale na
(the) shirt and jumped over (the) full sea but on

druhé straně si trochu namočil nohu. Kurent
(the) other side himself a little soaked (the) leg Kurent

se tomu zasmál a začal člověka popichovat.
himself at this laughed and started man to taunt

Člověk ale mlčel, jen vykročil a přešel
Man however became silent only stepped back and went to

celé moře jako přes malý potok – a vůbec
full sea as over (a) small stream – and at all

si přitom nenamočil nohy.
himself while not got wet (the) feet

„Já vyhrál!“ zvolal člověk a ukázal na své
I won exclaimed man and (he) showed at his

suché nohy.
dry feet

Kurent uznal porážku a řekl: „Dobře,
Kurent acknowledged defeat and said Good

člověče, roviny, moře i vše za ním
man (the) plains (the) sea and everything behind it

patří tobě. Ale to není všechno! Na zemi je toho
belong to you But this not is all On earth is this

ještě více. Pojď, uvidíme, kdo dokáže rozrazit zem
still more Go see who can break up ground

do větší hloubky."
to larger depths

Kurent vykročil na skálu, dupnul, až to zadunělo
Curent stepped on (a) rock stomped then it rang

jako hrom, a skála pukla. Vznikla hluboká
like thunder and (the) rock cracked Was created (a) deep

díra plná hadů. Potom dupnul člověk, až se
hole full of snakes Then stomped man until itself

celá země zatřásla. Prorazil puklinu až do
(the) whole earth shook Broke (a) crack until to

jádra zemë, kde tekla zlatá řeka, a
(the) core (of the) earth where flowed (a) golden river and

hadi popadali dolů a utopili se v
(the) snakes fell down and drowned themselves in

ní.
(of) her

Kurent mu uznal další vítězství: „Tohle je
Kurent him acknowledged further victory This is

taky tvoje, ale za vládce tě neuznám, dokud
also yours but for ruler you (I) don't recognize until

mě nepřemůžeš potřetí. Vidíš tu
me (you) can't beat for the third time (You) see this here

vysokou horu? Dosahuje až k nebesům. Tam
high mountain (It) reaches until to heaven There

nahoře sedí kohout, který hlídá boží jídlo. Kdo
above sits (a) rooster who guards (the) divine food Who

dostřelí střelou výš, získá celou zemi,
reaches (with their) shot above will obtain (the) entire earch

nebe i vše pod zemí."
heaven and all under (the) earth

Kurent vzal luk a střelil. Jeho střela letěla osm
Kurent took (a) bow and shot His arrow flew eight

dní a pak se vrátila zpět. Poté střelil člověk
days and then itself returned back Then shot man

a jeho střela letěla devět dní. Desátý den se
and his missile flew nine days (On the) tenth day itself

vrátila a na hrotu střely byl nabodnutý
returned and on (the) tip (of the) arrow was impaled

nebeský kohout.
(the) heavenly rooster

Kurent se poklonil a řekl: „Jsi carem!
Kurent himself complimented and said (You) are Tsar

Klaním se ti."
(I) bow myself to you

Člověk byl dobrosrdečný a rozhodl se s
Person was good-hearted and decided himself with

Kurentem	spřátelit.	Spolu	se	pak
Kurent	to make friends	Together	themselves	then

vydali,	aby	společně	spravovali	svět.
(they) gave out	in order that	together	(they) rule	(the) world
they went out				

Kurentovi	ale	vadilo,	že	prohrál,	a
(To) Kurent	however	(it) bothered	that	(he) lost	and

rozhodl	se	použít	chytrost.	„Jsi	sice
(he) decided	himself	to use	cleverness	(You) are	although
					maybe

silný,	člověče,"	říkal	si	pro	sebe,	„ale	vsadím
strong	man	(he) said	himself	for	himself	but	(I) bet

se,	že	jsi	také	důvěřivý."
myself	that	(you) are	also	gullible

Vyrobil	nápoj	z	červeného	vína	a	nabídl	ho
(He) made	(a) drink	from	red	wine	and	offered	it

člověku.	Když	ho	našel	na	druhé	straně
(to the) man	When	him	(he) found	on	(the) other	side of

moře,	jak	jí	kaši,	řekl	mu:	„Pane,	panuješ
(the) sea	as	(he) eats	porridge	(he) told	him	Lord	(you) reign

nad světem, ale piješ jen obyčejnou vodu? Zkus
over (the) world but drink only ordinary water Try

můj nápoj, připravil jsem ho speciálně pro tebe."
my drink prepared (I) am it especially for you
I have

Člověk se nechal přesvědčit a vypil pohár
Man himself let convince and drank (a) cup

vína. „Díky, Kurente, jsi laskavý. Tvůj nápoj je
(of) wine Thanks Kurent (you) are kind Your drink is

dobrý, ale voda je lepší," řekl a dál jedl
good but water is better (he) said and further ate

kaši. Kurent odcházel zamračený, ale nevzdal
porridge Kurent left frowning but didn't give up
vexed

se. Vyrobil další pohár vína a tentokrát
himself (He) made (an)other cup (of) wine and this time

do něj přidal čemeřici, magickou bylinu.
to it added hellebore (a) magic herb

Kurent se znovu vydal hledat člověka a
Kurent himself again gave out to search man and
directed

našel ho tentokrát na dně země, kde

(he) found him this time on (the) bottom (of the) earth where

tekla zlatá řeka. „Co děláš, pane?“ ptal se

flowed (the) golden river What (you) do lord asked himself

Kurent.

Kurent

„Tkám si zlatou košili, ale mám velkou žízeň,“

(I) weave myself (a) golden shirt but (I) have great thirst

odpověděl člověk.

answered man

„Mohu ti pomoci,“ řekl Kurent. „Vezmi si

(I) can you help said Kurent Take yourself

tento pohár, žádné slunce lepší víno nevidělo.“

this cup any sun better wine not saw

Člověk poděkoval, vzal číši a vypil. „Děkuji,

Man thanked took (a) glass and drank Thank you

Kurente. Tento tvůj nápoj je opravdu dobrý.“

Kurent This your drink is really good

Kurent	mu	chtěl	nalít	další,	ale	člověk	odmítl.
Kurent	him	wanted	to pour	further	but	man	rejected

Byl	od	přírody	střídmý	a	rozumný.	Kurent
(He) was	from	nature	frugal	and	reasonable	Kurent

odešel	ještě	víc	zamračený,	protože	viděl,	že
went	still	more	frowning vexed	because	(he) saw	that

člověk	nad	ním	stále	vítězí.	Vyrobil	tedy	víno
man	over	him	still	wins	(He) made	so	(a) wine

potřetí,	ale	tentokrát	do	něj	přidal	trochu
for the third time	but	this time	to	it	added	a little

vlastní	krve.
of his own	blood

Potřetí	našel	člověka	na	vysoké	hoře,
For the third time	(he) found	man	on	(a) high	mountain

jak	jí	pečeni	určenou	Bohu.	„Co	děláš,
how	(he) eats	roast	designated	(for) god	What	(you) do

pane?“	zeptal	se	Kurent	a	viděl,	že	člověk
lord	asked	himself	Kurent	and	saw	that	man

páchá těžký hřích.
commits (a) heavy sin

„Jím, ale mám strach, že přijde Bůh a ztrestá
(I) eat but (I) have fear that comes god and punishes

mě," odpověděl člověk.
me answered man

„Neboj se," řekl Kurent. „Tady máš víno,
Don't worry yourself said Kurent Here (you) have wine

které nikde jinde nenajdeš." Člověk se
which nowhere elsewhere (you) won't find Man himself

nechal potřetí přemluvit a vypil pohár. „Dej
let for the third time persuade and drank (a) cup Give

mi ještě jeden pohár, Kurente!" řekl radostně.
me still one cup Kurent (he) said joyfully

Vypil další pohár, až se mu zakalilo
(He) drank another cup then himself him blacked out

oko a ztratil paměť. Zapomněl dokonce
(the) eye and lost (the) memory Forgot even

na Boha a zůstal sedět u stolu.
about god and stayed to sit at (the) table

Když se Bůh vrátil a našel člověka, jak
When himself god returned and (he) found man how

jí jeho jídlo a usíná u jeho stolu,
(he) eats his food and falls asleep at his table

rozhněval se a silnou rukou ho svrhl
(he) angered himself and (with his) strong hand him toppled
threw

z hory. Člověk spadl dolů a zůstal ležet,
from (the) mountain Man dropped down and stayed lying

potlučený a oslabený.
battered and weakened

Když se po letech zotavil, už
When himself on years retrieved from already
years later he had recollected

neměl sílu. Nemohl ani přes moře, ani
(he) didn't have power Couldn't (go) neither over sea nor

do jádra země, ani na horu k
to (the) core (of the) earth nor on (the) mountain to

nebeskému stolu. Tak se stalo, že Kurent
(the) heavenly table Yes itself happened that Kurent

nakonec ovládl svět i člověka, který ztratil
finally dominated (the) world and man who lost

svou sílu a byl od té doby slabý a malý.
his power and (he) was from those times weak and small

O hloupém vlkovi

About (the) Foolish Wolf

Jednoho dne se vlkovi zdál zvláštní sen. V
One day itself (to the) wolf appeared (a) special dream In

tom snu dostal výbornou svačinu – jídlo,
this dream (he) acquired (an) excellent snack – food

o kterém mohl jen snít. Když se
about which (he) could only dream When himself

probudil, cítil se hladový a řekl si:
(he) woke up (he) felt himself hungry and told himself

„To by bylo, kdybych našel něco k
This would was if would (I) found something to
That would be something if I would find

snědku! Ale sny jsou nepolapitelné jako vítr.
eat But dreams are elusive as (the) wind

Říká se, že sny se neplní."
Says oneself that dreams themselves not fulfill
It is said don't come true

Vstal	ze	svého	brlohu,	protáhl	se	a
(He) stood up	from	his	den	stretched	himself	and

vydal	se	na	cestu	lesem.	Brzy	na
gave out directed	himself	on	(a) journay	(through the) forest	Soon	on

jedné	stezce	něco	zahlédl.	„Ale	co	to?“	řekl
one	trail	something	spotted	But	what	this	(he) said

si	překvapeně.	Na	zemi	ležel	velký	kus
himself	surprised	On	(the) ground	lay	(a) large	piece

sádla.	„No	ne,	tak	sny	se	asi	občas
(of) lard	Well	no	so	dreams	themselves	probably	occasionally

plní!“	řekl	radostně	a	rychle	začal	sádlo
fulfill come true!	(he) said	joyfully	and	quickly	started	(the) lard

jíst.	Polovinu	sádla	snědl	a	druhou	polovinu
to eat	Half	(the) lard	ate	and	(the) other	half

si	vzal	s	sebou	do	úkrytu.	„Když	mám
himself	took	with	himself	to	(his) shelter	When	(I) have

takové	štěstí,	kdo	ví,	co	dnes	ještě	najdu!“
such	luck	who	sees	what	today	still	(I) can find

pomyslel si a vydal se dál.
thought himself and gave out himself further
directed

Po chvíli přišel k louži, kde se pásla kobyla
On while (he) came to (a) pond where herself grazed (a) mare
time

se svým hříbětem. Vlk se na ně chvilku
with her foal (The) wolf himself at them a moment

díval a pak povídá: „Kobylko, sním ti to
looked at and then (he) says Little mare (I'll) eat (of) you this

hříbě!“
foal

Kobyla se na vlka podívala a odpověděla:
(The) mare herself at (the) wolf (she) looked and answered

„Ale vlku, jen si posluž. Mně to hříbě pořád
But wolf only yourself please To me this foal still
go ahead

jen kouše, sedlák mě nutí pracovat, a k tomu
only bites (the) farmer me forces to work and to this

všemu mě bolí noha. Moc bys mi pomohl,
to all me hurts (the) leg Much (you) would me helped

kdybys	mi	vytáhl	trn,	co	mě	píchá	v	noze.“
if you	me	got out	(the) thorn	what	me	sticks	in	(the) leg

Vlk	byl	překvapený.	„To	zní	snadně,“	řekl.
(The) wolf	was	surprised	This	sounds	easy	(he) said

„Ukaž,	kobylko,	pomůžu	ti!“
Show	little mare	I'll help	you

Kobyla	zvedla	zadní	nohu,	jako	by
(The) mare	picked up	(the) rear	leg	as if	(she) would

opravdu	čekala,	že	jí	vlk	pomůže.	Vlk
really	awaited	that	her	(the) wolf	helps	(The) wolf

se	sehnul,	aby	se	podíval	na
himself	approached	in order that	himself	(he) looked	at

kopyto.	V	tu	chvíli	ho	kobyla	prudce	kopla
(the) hoof	In	here	while	him	(the) mare	abruptly	kicked
		this	time				

přímo	do	čumáku!	Vlk	udělal	kotrmelec	a
directly	to	(the) snout	(The) wolf	made	(a) somersault	and

zůstal	chvíli	omráčeně	ležet.	Když	se
stayed	(a) while	stunned	lying	When	himself

vzpamatoval a rozhlédl se, kobyla s
(he) recovered and looked around himself (the) mare with

hříbětem už byla pryč.
(her) foal already was off

„Tedy, to jsem se nechal napálit,“ zamumlal vlk
So that (I) am myself let dupe muttered wolf

a vydal se dál.
and directed himself further

Brzy potkal na své cestě prasnici se skupinkou
Soon (he) met on his road (a) sow with (a) group

malých prasátek. „Prasnice, sním ti všechna
(of) small piglets Sow (I'll) eat you all

prasátka!“ oznámil vlk s nadějí, že tentokrát
piglets announced (the) wolf with hope that this time

si pochutná.
himself snacks

Prasnice se však usmála a odpověděla: „To
(The) sow herself however (she) smiled and answered This

by mi moc pomohlo, vlku. Ta prasátka mě
would me much helped wolf These piglets me

pořád hryžou a nemám na ně sílu. Ale
still bite and (I) have not for them strength But

víš, že ještě nejsou pokřtěná? Musíme
(you) know that still not (they are) christened (We) must

je nejdřív pokřtít!“
them first christen

Vlk se zamyslel. „Dobře,“ řekl nakonec.
(The) wolf himself thought Good (he) said finally

„Pojďme je pokřtít k řece.“
Let go us them christen to (the) river

Šli tedy spolu k řece. Prasátka však
(They) went so together to (the) river (The) piglets however

začala nahlas kvičet. Kvikot byl tak hlasitý,
started out loud to squeal (The) squealing was so loud

že ho uslyšeli strážní psi z nedalekého
that it (they) heard (the) guard dogs from (the) nearby

mlýna. Brzy přiběhli k řece a vrhli
mill Soon (they) came running to (the) river and rushed

se na vlka. Prasnice v té chvíli vzala
themselves at (the) wolf (The) sow in that time (she) took

poslední prasátko a utekla. Psi vlka
(the) last piggy and escaped (The) dogs (the) wolf
all the piglets

pokousali tak, že z něj visely hadry, ale
bit so that from him hung rags but

nakonec se jim podařilo utéct.
finally himself them succeeded to escape

„To snad není možné," bručel vlk, když se
This perhaps not is possible grumbled (the) wolf when himself

vzpamatoval a otřepával se. „Dnes mám
(he) recovered and shook himself Today (I) have

vážně smůlu. Ale jednou se mi snad poštěstí!"
seriously bad luck But once myself me perhaps am lucky

řekl si a pokračoval dál.
(he) said himself and continued further

Dostal se až na vysokou horu, kde našel
Got himself then on (a) high mountain where (he) found
He arrived

stádo koz. Rozhlédl se a prohlásil: „Kozy,
(a) herd (of) goats Look around himself and (he) stated Goats

já vás všechny sním!“
I you all eat

Kozy se ale jen zasmály a odpověděly: „Sněz
Goats himself but only laughed and answered by Eat

nás, ale nech nás se nejdřív pomodlit, než
us but leave us ourselves first (to) pray until
before

umřeme.“
(we) die

Vlk zamyšleně kývl hlavou. „Dobře,
(The) wolf thoughtfully nodded (the) head Good

pomodlete se, ale rychle!“
(you) pray yourselves but quickly

Kozy se postavily do řady a začaly
Goats themselves built by to rows and (they) started

se modlit růženec. „Ahú, ahú, ahú!“
themselves to pray (the) rosary Ahoy ahoy ahoy

opakovaly a vlk se k nim přidal. V tu chvíli
repeated and wolf himself to them added In here while

jejich modlení uslyšel ovčácký pes, který
their praying heard (a) sheep- dog who

hory hlídal. Přiběhl k vlkovi a s chutí
(the) mountain guarded (He) ran to (the) wolf and with taste
pleasure

se do něj zakousl. Psi z mlýna ho sice
himself to him bit Dogs from (the) mill him although
maybe

pokousali, ale tenhle pes byl ještě silnější.
bit but this one dog was still stronger
they had bitten (well)

Vlkovi nezůstalo na těle ani jedno místo
(The) wolf not left on (the) body not one place

bez rány, a tak opět zůstal ležet a
without wounds and yes again remained lying and

odpočíval.
rested

„Proč mám dnes takovou smůlu?“ ptal se
Why (I) have today such bad luck asked himself

vlk sám sebe. Ale po chvíli se zvedl,
(the) wolf self himself But after (a) while himself (he) picked up

otřel prach ze srsti a vydal se dál.
wiped (the) dust from (the) fur and directed himself further

Nakonec došel k louce, kde se pásl
Finally (he) reached to (the) meadow where himself pastured

starý beran. Vlk se na něj podíval a řekl:
(the) old ram (The) wolf himself at him looked and said

„Berane, já tě sním!“
Ram I you eat

Beran se na něj klidně podíval a odpověděl:
(The) ram himself at him calmly looked and answered

„Sněz mě, vlku, už jsem starý. Ale co bys
Eat me wolf already (I) am old But what would you

z toho měl? Jen si zkazíš zuby.
from this had have Only yourself (you'll) ruin (the) teeth

Víš co? Postav se dole a otevři
You know what Lay yourself down and open

pusu, já ti skočím rovnou do tlamy.“
(your) mouth I you (will) jump straight into (the) mouth (animal)

Vlk se zamyslel, ale pak se ušklíbl. „To
(The) wolf himself thought but then himself grinned This

je dobrý nápad!“ řekl, slezl z kopce, otevřel
is (a) good idea (he) said went down hill opened

pusu a čekal. Beran se rozběhl, sklonil hlavu
half and waited Ram himself ran bowed head

a vší silou vlka nabral. Vlk odletěl,
and all by force (the) wolf scooped up (The) wolf flew away

převalil se a zůstal ležet napůl mrtvý.
rolled over himself and stayed lying half dead

Po dlouhé době se vlk zvedl a klopýtal
After (a) long time himself (the) wolf picked up and stumbled

dál, sotva držel rovnováhu. Nakonec dorazil
further (he) barely held (the) balance Finally (he) arrived

k velkému dubu a posadil se pod něj.
to (a) great oak and sat himself under him

„Jaký jsem to hlupák," řekl si smutně. „Věřil
How (I) am this stupid (he) said himself sadly Believed

jsem, že se mi splní sen o
(I) am that himself me (it) will fulfill (a) dream about

úžasné svačině, ale místo toho jsem si
(an) amazing snack but (in) place (of) this (I) am myself

nadělal jen problémy. Nechat se obelstít
made only problems Let myself trick

kobylou, prasnicí, modlil se s kozami, věřil
(the) mare (the) sow prayed myself with (the) goats believed

beranovi... jsem opravdu hloupý."
(the) ram (I) am really stupid

V tu chvíli se za dubem objevil sedlák s
In this time itself behind (the) oak appeared (a) farmer with

ostrou sekyrou. Slyšel vlkovy nářky a
(a) sharp axe (He) heard (the) wolf's lamentations and

rozhodl se mu „pomoci“. Bác! Sekl a sťal
decided himself him to help Whack (He) slashed and cut

vlkovi ocas.
(the) wolf's tail

Od té doby vlk běhá lesem bez ocasu.
From that time (the) wolf runs (the) woods without tail

A jestli ještě neumřel, možná tam běhá dodnes.
And if (he) still (is) undead maybe there runs to this day
didn't die

Obuchu, hýbej se!
Club, Move Yourself

Jednoho	sobotního	večera	seděl	švec	a
One	Saturday	evening	sat	(a) cobbler	and

opravoval	staré	boty.	Chtěl	mít	boty
(he) repaired	old	shoes	(He) wanted	to have	(the) shoes

hotové	na	neděli,	aby	v	nich	mohl	jít	do
finished	on	Sunday	in order that	in	them	(he) could	go	to

kostela.	Pracoval	dlouho	do	noci,	a	když
church	He worked	long	to	(the) night	and	when

konečně	skončil,	vydechl	si	a	řekl:
finally	(he) finished	(he) breathed out	-himself-	and	said
		he breathed deeply			

„Už	to	mám	hotové.	Teď	se	můžu	slušně
Already	this	(I) have	finished	Now	myself	(I) can	decently

obléknout	a	v	klidu	jít	na	mši.“
dress up	and	in	calmness	go	to	mass
		at	ease			

V	neděli	ráno	se	švec	vydal	do
In	Sunday	morning	himself	(the) cobbler	gave out directed	to

kostela,	kde	slyšel	kázání	kněze.
(the) church	where	(he) heard	(the) sermon	(of the) priest

Kněz	říkal:	„Kdo	obětuje	své	jmění	kostelu,
(The) priest	said	Who	sacrifices	his	assets	(to the) church

tomu	Bůh	stonásobně	vrátí.	A	nejen	to!	Bůh
this one	god	(a) hundredfold	returns	And	not only	this	God

pomůže	i	v	dalších	věcech."	Švec	byl
helps	also	in	(the) next	things	(The) cobbler	was

chudý	a	tahle	slova	na	něj	udělala	velký
poor	and	these	words	on	him	made	(a) great

dojem.	Pomyslel	si:	„Možná	je	to	moje
impression	(He) thought	(by) himself	Maybe	is	this	my

šance.	Prodat	svůj	dům	i	nástroje	a	věnovat
chance	To sell	my	house	and	tools	and	dedicate

vše	kostelu.	Třeba	se	potom	Bůh	postará
all	(to the) church	Possibly	himself	then	god	will take care

o mě i moji rodinu.“
of me and my family

Jakmile se vrátil domů, řekl ženě o
As soon as himself returned home (he) told (his) wife about

svém plánu. „Cože?!“ vykřikla žena, „Chceš
his plan What exclaimed (the) wife (You) want

prodat naši chalupu i všechen náš majetek?
to sell our cottage and all our property

Vždyť je to naše živobytí!“
After all is this our livelihood

„Ano, ženo,“ odpověděl švec. „Kněz říkal,
Yes wife answered (the) cobbler (The) priest said

že Bůh nám všechno vrátí, a možná i víc.
that god us all returns and maybe also more

Musíme věřit.“
(We) must trust

Žena nevěřila svým uším, ale švec byl
(The) woman didn't believe her ears but (the) cobbler was

rozhodnutý. Prodali chalupu a nářadí a
resolved (They) sold (the) cottage and tools and

peníze odevzdali knězi na kostel. Pak
money handed over (to the) priest for (the) church Then

čekali, že se stane zázrak. Dny plynuly,
(they) waited that itself happens (a) miracle (The) days flowed by

ale nic se nedělo. Peníze rychle mizely,
but nothing itself happened (The) money quickly disappeared

děti plakaly hlady a žena se
(the) children cried hungrily and (the) woman herself

zlobila. „Vidíš?“ vyčítala ševci, „Teď
was angry (You) see (she) reproached (the) shoemaker Now

nemáme ani kde bydlet! A Bůh ti zatím
(we) have nothing neither where to live And god you so far

nic nevrátil.“
nothing not returned

Švec si nakonec řekl, že musí zjistit,
(The) cobbler himself finally said that (he) must find out

co se děje. Oblékl se jako žebrák,

what itself (is) happening (He) dressed himself like (a) beggar

vzal do ruky hůl a vydal se hledat

took into (the) hand (a) stick and gave out himself to search

Boha. „Snad mi Bůh vysvětlí, proč nás nechal v

god Perhaps me god will explain why us (he) left in

nesnázích," říkal si po cestě. Šel celé

predicament (he) told himself on (the) road (He) went (a) full

dny a celé noci a nakonec narazil na

day and (a) full night and finally came across on

starého pastýře, který pásl velké stádo ovcí.

(an) old shepherd who pastured (a) great herd (of) sheep

Pastýř si ševce všiml a zavolal

(The) shepherd himself (the) shoemaker spotted and (he) called

na něj: „Pojď sem, člověče. Vypadáš hladově. Mám

to him Go here man (You) look hungry (I) have

tu trochu jídla, podělím se s tebou."

here a little food I'll share myself with you

Švec poděkoval a usedl k pastýři.
(The) cobbler thanked and sat down (next) to (the) shepherd

Během jídla mu vyprávěl svůj příběh – o
During (the) meal him (he) told his story - about

tom, jak všechno obětoval kostelu, ale Bůh
this how everything (he) sacrificed (to the) church but god

mu zatím nic nevrátil. Starý pastýř se
him so far nothing not returned (The) old shepherd himself

nad ním slitoval a řekl: „Mám pro tebe něco
over him had mercy and said (I) have for you something

zvláštního. Dám ti tohoto beránka. Když
special (I) will give you this lamb When

řekneš: ‚Beránku, otřes se,' začne z něj padat
(you) say Lamb shake yourself starts from him to fall

zlato. Ale dám ti jednu radu – vyhni se
gold But (I) will give you one advice - avoid yourself

hospodě u tvé kmotry."
(the) inn at your godmother's

Švec byl nadšený, poděkoval pastýři a
(The) cobbler was enthusiastic thanked (the) shepherd and

vydal se domů s beránkem na rameni.
directed himself home with (the) lamb on (the) shoulders

Když byl trochu dál od pastýře, pomyslel
When (he) was a little further from (the) shepherd thought

si: „Opravdu z obyčejného beránka padají
by himself Really from (an) ordinary lamb fall

dukáty? Musím to zkusit!“ Postavil beránka na
ducats I have to this try (He) set (the) lamb on

zem a zkusil slova, co mu řekl
(the) ground and tried (the) words that him told

pastýř: „Beránku, otřes se!“
(the) shepherd Lamb shake yourself

K jeho údivu začaly z beránka padat
To his astonishment (they) started from lamb to fall

zlaté dukáty. „To je neuvěřitelné!“ vykřikl
golden ducats This is unbelievable (he) exclaimed

radostně. Vzal beránka na ramena a vydal
joyfully (He) took (the) lamb on (the) shoulders and directed

se domů, plný naděje. Když procházel kolem
himself home full (of) hope When passing through by

hospody, kde bydlela jeho kmotra, vyběhla
(the) inn where lived his godmother (she) ran out

ven. „Milý kmotře, pojď na chvilku dovnitř! Už
outside Dear godson go for a moment inside Already

jsme se tak dlouho neviděli," přemlouvala
(we) are each other so long not seen (she) coaxed

ho.
him

Švec si vzpomněl na varování, ale pak si
Cobbler himself remembered on (the) warning but then himself

řekl, že se nic nestane, když se na
said that himself nothing will not happen when himself for

chvíli zastaví. „Dobře, kmotřičko, ale dám ti
(a) while stops Good godmother but (I) will give you

tohohle beránka na chvilku schovat. Ale neříkej:
this one lamb for a moment to hide But don't say

‚Beránku, otřes se!‘ To by ho mohlo vyděsit.“
(The) lamb shake yourself This would him could scare

Kmotra se usmála a kývla. Jakmile
(The) godmother -herself- smiled and nods As soon as

však švec odešel, zvědavost jí nedala
however (the) cobbler went curiosity her didn't give
couldn't hold in

a zkusila říct: „Beránku, otřes se!“ A
and (she) tried to say Lamb shake yourself And

opravdu, začaly z něj padat dukáty.
really (they) started from it to fall ducats

Kmotra si vymyslela plán, jak svého
(The) godmother herself invented (a) plan how her

kmotra ošidit. Opila ho, a když usnul, vyměnila
godson to cheat Got drunk him and when asleep replaced

beránka za obyčejného.
(the) lamb for (an) ordinary

Ráno	se	švec	probudil,	vzal
(In the) morning	himself	(the) cobbler	(he) woke up	took

„beránka“	a	šel	domů.	Byl	nadšený,	že
(the) lamb	and	(he) went	home	(He) was	enthusiastic	that

děti	nakrmí,	a	sotva	dorazil,	řekl
(the) children	(he) will feed	and	barely	arrived	(he) said

radostně:	„Beránku,	otřes	se!“	Ale	nic	se
joyfully	Lamb	shake	yourself	But	nothing	itself

nestalo.	Beránek	stál	a	ani	se	nehnul.
did not happen	(The) lamb	stood	and	neither	itself	moved

„Co	je	to	za	trik?“	divil	se	švec.
What	is	this	for	trick	wondered	himself	(the) cobbler

Zkoušel	to	znovu,	ale	stále	nic.	Děti
(He) tried	this	again	but	still	nothing	(The) children

se	mu	začaly	smát	a	žena	ho
themselves	(of) him	started	to laugh	and	(the) woman	him

nazvala	bláznem.	Zklamaný	švec	pochopil,	že
called	(a) fool	Disappointed	(the) cobbler	understood	that

ho kmotra ošidila, a vydal se znovu za
him (the) godmother cheated and directed himself again for

pastýřem.
(the) shepherd

Pastýř ho vyslechl a rozhodl se mu
(The) shepherd him heard out and decided himself him

dát druhou šanci. „Dám ti tento kouzelný
to give (an)other chance (I) will give you this magical

ubrousek. Když řekneš: ‚Ubrousku, prostři se!‘,
napkin When (you) say Napkin set yourself

objeví se na něm jídlo. Ale znovu se vyhni
appears itself on him food But again yourself avoid

hospodě.“
(the) inn

Švec poděkoval a vydal se domů. Když
Cobbler thanked and directed himself home When

šel kolem hospody, kmotra už čekala.
(he) went by (the) inn (the) godmother already awaited

„Milý kmotře, pojď dovnitř!“ přemlouvala ho.
Dear godson go inside coaxed him

Švec se zdráhal, ale nakonec se nechal
(The) cobbler himself hesitated but finally himself let

přemluvit. Kmotře dal ubrousek a
persuade (To the) godmother (he) gave (the) napkin and

varoval ji: „Neříkej: ‚Ubrousku, prostři se!‘“ Ale
warned her Don't say Napkin set yourself But

jakmile odešel, kmotra to hned zkusila a
as soon as (he) went (the) godmother this now tried and

ubrousek se prostřel jídlem.
(the) napkin itself set (with) food

I tentokrát kmotra ševce opila a
Also this time (the) godmother (the) shoemaker got drunk and

vyměnila kouzelný ubrousek za obyčejný.
replaced (the) magical napkin for (a) common one

Švec šel domů s falešným ubrouskem,
(The) shoemaker went home with (the) fake napkin

řekl „Ubrousku, prostři se!“, ale nic se
said Napkin set yourself but nothing itself

nestalo. Rozzuřený pochopil, že ho
did not happen Furious (he) understood that him

kmotra znovu obelstila.
(the) godmother again deceived

Vydal se potřetí za pastýřem a
(He) directed himself for the third time for (the) shepherd and

prosil o další pomoc. Pastýř už byl
asked about further help (The) shepherd already was

rozhněvaný, ale nakonec mu dal kouzelnou hůl a
angry but finally him gave (a) magic stick and

řekl: „Když řekneš ‚Obuchu, hýbej se!‘, objeví
said When (you) say Stick move yourself appear

se dva silní muži a dají pořádný
themselves two strong men and (they) give (a) proper

výprask každému, koho si budeš přát. Až
spanking to everyone whom yourself (you) will wish Then

půjdeš kolem kmotry, zkus to na ni.“
(you) go around (to the) godmother try this on her

Švec poděkoval a vyrazil. Jakmile přišel
(The) cobbler thanked (him) and set off As soon as (he) came

ke kmotře, přivítala ho s úsměvem,
to (the) godmother (she) welcomed him with smile

netušíc, co se chystá. Švec jí dal
unknowing what itself was forthcoming (The) cobbler her gave

hůl a varoval: „Jen neříkej ‚Obuchu, hýbej
(the) stick and warned Only don't say Stick move

se!‘“ Ale kmotra, zvědavá jako vždy, šla do
yourself But (the) godmother curious as always went to

vedlejší místnosti a vyzkoušela to. Okamžitě se
(the) next room and tried this Immediately itself

objevili dva silní muži a začali ji mlátit.
appeared two strong men and started her to beat

Švec za dveřmi poslouchal křik a
(The) cobbler behind (the) door listened to (the) screams and

přikázal: „Obuchu, hýbej se, dokud mi
ordered Stick move yourself until me

kmotra nevrátí mého beránka a
(the) godmother will not return my lamb and

ubrousek!“ Kmotra v bolestech slíbila, že
napkin (The) godmother in pain promised that

mu všechno vrátí. Jakmile dostal zpátky své
him everything returns As soon as (he) acquired back his

věci, zvolal: „Obuchu, dost!“ Muži zmizeli
things (he) exclaimed Stick enough (The) men disappeared

a potlučená kmotra si odnesla svou lekci.
and (the) battered godmother herself took away learned her lesson

Švec se vrátil domů, kde jeho rodina
(The) cobbler himself returned home where his family

konečně měla dost peněz i jídla. Od té doby
finally had enough money and meals From that time

nikdy nezapomněl na moudrou radu – obcházet
never (he) not forgot on (the) wise advice – to bypass

nečestné lidi a vážit si toho, co
dishonest people and weigh themselves this what
value

mají.
(they) have

O žabce královně
About (the) Frog Queen

Byl	jednou	jeden	moudrý	král,	který	měl	tři
(There) was	once	a	wise	king	who	had	three

syny.	Když	uviděl,	že	jeho	synové	jsou	už
sons	When	(he) saw	that	his	sons	are	already

dospělí,	rozhodl	se,	že	jim	pomůže	najít
adults	(he) decided	himself	that	them	(he) helps	to find

nevěsty.	Jednoho	dne	si	je	tedy	předvolal	a
brides	One	day	himself	them	so	summoned	and

povídá:	„Synové	moji,	je	na	čase,	abyste
(he) says	Sons	(of) mine	(it) is	-on-	time	so that you

se	oženili.	Každý	z	vás	si	vezme	luk
yourself	married	Each	from	you	himself	takes	(a) bow

a	šíp,	půjde	na	zakázaná	luka	a	vystřelí
and	(an) arrow	go	on	(the) forbidden	meadow	and	fire

do různých stran. Tam, kam šíp dopadne,
in different directions There where (the) arrow turns out

tam se vydáte pro svou nevěstu."
there yourself give out for your bride
direct

Synové přikývli a vyrazili na zakázaná luka.
(The) sons nodded and went out on (the) forbidden meadow
acquiesced

Nejstarší bratr vystřelil šíp doprava,
(The) oldest brother fired (an) arrow to (the) right

prostřední doleva a nejmladší syn, bohatýr
(the) middle (son) to (the) left and (the) youngest son (the) hero

Ivan, vystřelil šíp přímo před sebe. Potom
Ivan fired (an) arrow directly in front of himself Then

se každý vydal hledat svůj šíp.
themselves each gave out to search their arrow
directed

Nejstarší bratr našel svůj šíp u domu
(The) oldest brother found his arrow at (the) house

ministra, vzal si tedy za ženu ministrovu
(of the) minister took himself so for wife (the) minister's

dceru. Prostřední bratr našel šíp u
daughter (The) middle brother found (the) arrow at

generála a vzal si za ženu jeho krásnou
(the) general and took himself for wife his beautiful

dceru. Ivan ale hledal dlouho a šíp
daughter Ivan however searched long but (the) arrow

nikde nemohl najít. Prošel celé lesy a
nowhere couldn't find (He) went through all forests and

všechny hory, až třetího dne došel do
all mountains then (at the) third day (he) reached to

bahnitého močálu. Tam konečně zahlédl svůj
(a) muddy swamp There finally (he) spotted his

šíp – držela ho v tlamě velká žába.
arrow – held him in (the) mouth (a) large frog

„Ach jo," povzdechl si Ivan. „Mám si za
Ah yeah sighed (by) himself Ivan (I) have myself for

nevěstu vzít žábu?" Chtěl odejít, ale vtom
bride to take (a) frog (He) wanted to leave but in-that

žabka zavolala: „Kvak, kvak! Bohatýre Ivane, pojď
(the) frog called Quack quack Hero Ivan go

sem ke mně a vezmi si svůj šíp. Jinak
here to me and take yourself your arrow Otherwise

se z tohoto bahna nikdy nedostaneš!“
yourself from this mud never (you) won't get

Ivan byl překvapený, že žába mluví, ale poslechl
Ivan was surprised that (the) frog talks but listened to

ji. Jakmile se přiblížil, žabka se
her As soon as himself (he) approached (the) frog herself

přetočila a najednou se kolem ní objevila
spun around and at once itself around (of) her appeared

krásná hostina. „Vím, že jsi dlouho bloudil,“
(a) beautiful banquet (I) know that (you) are you have long wandered

řekla žabka. „Musíš být hladový. Pojď blíž, mám
said (the) frog (You) must be hungry Come closer (I) have

pro tebe něco k jídlu.“
for you something to eat

Ivan tedy vešel a hned před sebou uviděl

Ivan thus (he) went and now before himself (he) saw

krásně prostřený stůl s jídlem a pitím.

(a) beautifully set table with food and drink

Byl unavený a hladový, a tak se posadil

(He) was tired and hungry and so himself sat down

a pořádně se najedl. Když skončil, žabka

and properly himself fed When (he) finished (the) frog

mu povídá: „Tvoje střela dopadla ke mně, a

him says Your arrow hit to me and

proto si mě musíš vzít za ženu. Když si

therefore yourself me must take for (a) wife When yourself

mě nevezmeš, zůstaneš v této bažině navždy.“

me (you) don't take (you)'ll stay in this swamp forever

Ivan nevěděl, co má dělat. Ale nakonec se

Ivan didn't know what (he) has to do But finally himself

rozhodl žabku poslechnout. Vzal ji do

(he) decided (the) frog to listen to (He) took her by

rukou	a	odnesl	domů.	Jeho	bratři	a	jejich
(the) hand	and	brought away	to home	His	brothers	and	their

krásné	nevěsty	se	mu	hned	začali	smát.
beautiful	brides	themselves	(at) him	now	started	to laugh

„Podívejte,	Ivan	si	přivedl	nevěstu	–	žábu!“
See (you all)	Ivan	himself	brought	(a) bride	–	(a) frog

posmívali	se	mu.
mocked	themselves	him

Přišel	den	svatby.	Nejstarší	a	prostřední
Came	(the) day	(of the) wedding	(The) oldest	and	middle

bratr	jeli	na	svatbu	v	krásných	kočárech,
brother	went	to	(the) wedding	in	beautiful	carriages

každý	se	svou	nevěstou.	Ivan	jel	v	kočáře
each	with	his	bride	Ivan	rode	in	(a) carriage

sám	a	žabku	nesl	na	zlaté	míse.	Když	pak
himself	and	(the) frog	carried	in	(a) golden	bowl	When	then

nadešla	svatební	noc	a	Ivan	zůstal	s
arrived	(the) wedding	night	and	Ivan	stayed	with

nevěstou o samotě, žabka si sundala svou
(the) bride on solitude (the) frog herself took down her

kůži a proměnila se v nádhernou dívku.
skin and (she) turned herself in (a) beautiful girl

Byla krásnější než obě nevěsty dohromady.
(She) was more beautiful than both brides together

Ale ráno si opět oblékla žabí kůži
But (in the) morning herself again dressed (into the) frog skin

a celý den vypadala jako obyčejná žába.
and (the) whole day looked like (a) common frog

Brzy nato král zavolal své syny a řekl jim:
Soon then (the) king called his sons and told them

„Teď jste už všichni ženatí, a tak bych
Now (you) are already all married and so (I) would

rád viděl, jak šikovné jsou vaše ženy. Ať mi
gladly saw how handy are your women Let to me

každá z nich do zítřka ušije košili.“ Každému
each from them until tomorrow sew (a) shirt (To) every

synovi dal kus látky a oni ho přinesli
son (he) gave (a) piece (of) cloth and they it brought to

svým ženám.
their women

Nevěsty starších bratrů si hned svolaly
(The) brides (of the) elder brothers themselves now convened by

pomocnice a ty začaly košili šít. Služky
helpers and those started (the) shirt to sew (The) maids

začaly stříhat a šít, aby práce byla rychle
started to cut and sew in order that (the) work was quickly

hotová. Mezitím poslaly sluhu, aby zjistil,
ready Meanwhile (they) sent (a) servant in order that (he) found

co dělá Ivanova žabka. Když služka přišla do
what does Ivan's frog When (the) maid came to

Ivanovy komnaty, uviděla ho, jak smutně sedí.
Ivan's chambers (she) saw him how sadly (he) sits

„Proč jsi smutný, bohatýre Ivane?“ zeptala se
Why (you) are sad hero Ivan asked from

ho žabka.
him (the) frog

Ivan odpověděl: „Otec chce, abys mu do
Ivan answered Father wants in order that him by

zítřka ušila košili z této látky."
tomorrow (you) sewed (a) shirt from this cloth

Žabka se usmála a řekla: „Neměj starosti,
(The) frog herself smiled and said Don't have worry

běž si lehnout, všechno zařídím." Pak
go yourself lie down all (I) will arrange Then

vzala nůžky, rozstříhala plátno na malé kousky,
(she) took scissors cut (the) canvas in small pieces

otevřela okno a vyhodila je ven. Zavolala:
opened (the) window and threw them out (She) called

„Silní větrové, rozneste tyto kousky a ušijte mi
Strong wind spread these pieces and sew me

krásnou košili pro krále."
(a) beautiful shirt for (the) king

Když	to	služka	viděla,	běžela	to	povědět
When	this	(the) maid	saw	(she) ran	this	to tell

nevěstám	starších	bratrů.	„Ta	žába	je	blázen!“
(the) brides	(of the) elder	brothers	This	frog	is	crazy

smály	se.	„Co	asi	její	muž	přinese
(they) laughed	themselves	What	maybe	her	man	will bring
			do you think			

zítra	králi?“
tomorrow	(to the) king

Ráno,	když	se	Ivan	probudil,	našel	vedle
Morning	when	himself	Ivan	woke up	(he) found	next to

sebe	překrásnou	košili.	Žabka	mu	řekla:	„Vezmi
himself	(a) beautiful	shirt	(The) frog	him	said	Take

tuhle	košili	a	předej	ji	svému	otci.“	Ivan	tedy
here	shirt	and	pass on	her	to your	father	Ivan	so

přinesl	košili	do	trůnního	sálu	a	bratři
brought	(the) shirt	to	(the) throne	hall	and	(the) brothers

také	přinesli	ty	své.
also	brought	those	of them

Král si nejprve prohlédl košili od
(The) king himself first viewed (the) shirt from

nejstaršího syna a řekl: „Tahle je docela
(the) oldest son and said This one is quite

obyčejná.“ Pak se podíval na košili
common Then himself (he) looked at (the) shirt

prostředního syna: „Tahle je také obyčejná.“
(of the) middle son This one is also common

Nakonec vzal do rukou košili od Ivana a
Finally (he) took to hand (the) shirt from Ivan and

divil se, jak je krásná. „Tuhle košili si
wondered himself how she is beautiful This here shirt itself

budu oblékat jen při zvláštních příležitostech!“
(I) will dress only at special opportunities

rozhodl.
(he) decided

O několik dní později dal král synům
About several days later gave (the) king (the) sons

další úkol. „Milí synové," řekl, „rád bych
(a) further task Dear sons (he) said gladly (I) would

zjistil, jestli vaše ženy umí také vyšívat zlatem
found if your women can also embroider with gold

a stříbrem. Přineste jim stříbro, zlato a
and silver Bring them silver gold and

hedvábí, a každá ať mi do zítřka vyšije
silk and each let me by tomorrow sew

koberec."
(a) carpet

Bratři opět odnesli materiály svým ženám.
(The) brothers again took away (the) materials to their women

Nevěsty starších bratrů si hned zavolaly
(The) brides (of the) elder brothers themselves now called

komorné a další pomocnice, aby jim
chambermaids and further helpers in order that them

s prací pomohly. Ty se pustily do
with (the) work (they) help Those themselves let go to
started on

vyšívání	–	některé	stříbrem,	jiné	zlatem.
(the) embroidery	–	some	(with) silver	others	(with) gold

Mezitím	opět	poslaly	služku,	aby	zjistila,
Meanwhile	again	(they) sent	(the) maid	in order that	(she) found

co	bude	dělat	Ivanova	žabka.	Ivan	byl	znovu
what	will	do	Ivan's	frog	Ivan	was	again

velmi	smutný.	„Proč	jsi	tak	smutný,	bohatýre
very	sad	Why	(you) are	so	sad	hero

Ivane?“	zeptala	se	ho	žabka.	„Jak	bych	nebyl
Ivan	asked	from	him	(the) frog	How	would	(I) not be

smutný?“	odpověděl	Ivan.	„Otec	si	přeje,
sad	answered	Ivan	Father	himself	wishes

abys	mu	do	zítřka	vyšila	koberec	z
that would	him	by	tomorrow	(an) embroidered	carpet	from

tohoto	zlata,	stříbra	a	hedvábí.“
this	gold	silver	and	silk

Žabka	se	na	něj	povzbudivě	usmála.	„Neměj
(The) frog	herself	at	him	encouragingly	smiled	Don't have

starost,"	řekla.	„Běž	spát,	je	moudřejší
concern	(she) said	Run	(to) sleep	is	wiser
				one is	

večera."
(in the) evening

Když	Ivan	usnul,	vzala	žabka	hedvábí,	stříbro	a
When	Ivan	slept	took	(the) frog	(the) silk	(the) silver	and

zlato,	rozstříhala	je	na	malé	kousky	a
(the) gold	cut	them	on	small	pieces	and

vyhodila	je	oknem.	Potom	zavolala:	„Silní
threw	them	(through the) window	Then	(she) called	Strong

větrové,	přineste	mi	koberec,	který	je	hodný
wind	bring	me	(a) carpet	which	is	worthy

krále."
(for a) king

Ráno	předala	žabka	Ivanovi	krásný
(In the) morning	gave over	(the) frog	(to) Ivan	(a) beautiful

koberec,	nádherně	vyšívaný,	jaký	král	ještě
carpet	beautifully	embroidered	as	(the) king	still

nikdy neviděl.
never not saw

Král si znovu zavolal syny a řekl jim:
(The) king himself again called (the) sons and told them

„Milí synové, tentokrát bych rád viděl, jak vaše
Dear sons this time (I) would gladly saw how your

ženy zvládnou upéct chléb. Ať každá upeče
women can handle to bake bread Let each one bake

bochník a zítra mi ho přineste.“
(a) loaf and tomorrow me it bring

Starší bratři okamžitě předali úkol svým
(The) older brothers immediately gave over (the) task to their

manželkám. Ty se hned pustily do práce,
wives Those themselves now set to work

ale zároveň poslaly služku zjistit, co bude
but simultaneously sent (the) maid to find out what will

dělat Ivanova žabka. Mezitím přišel Ivan do svých
do Ivan's frog Meanwhile came Ivan to his

komnat s plnou náručí mouky a vypadal
chamber with full arms (of) flour and looked

ustaraně.
worried

Žabka si toho všimla a hned se ho ptá:
(The) frog herself this noticed and now herself him asks

„Kvak, kvak! Proč jsi tak smutný, bohatýre
Quack quack Why are (you) so sad hero

Ivane?“
Ivan

„Otec chce, abys mu do zítřka upekla
Father wants that would him by tomorrow (you) baked

chléb,“ odpověděl Ivan.
(a) bread answered Ivan

Žabka se usmála a řekla: „Neměj žádné
(The) frog herself smiled and said Don't have any

starosti. Vše udělám, jen se jdi v klidu
worry All (I) will do only yourself go in calmness

vyspat.“ Vzala mouku, přilila do ní vodu,
sleep (She) took (the) flour added to her water

zadělala těsto a vylila ho do studené pece.
(she) made dough and poured out it into (the) cold furnace

Pak zavolala: „Ať se upeče chléb měkký, kyprý
Then called Let itself bake (the) bread soft plump

a bílý jako sníh!“
and white as snow

Služka, která vše pozorovala, běžela zpět k
(The) maid who all (that) observed ran back to

nevěstám starších bratrů. „Král si žabku
(the) brides (of the) elder brothers (The) king himself (the) frog

chválí, ale ona nic neumí! Vždyť ani
praises but she nothing can't After all neither

neroztopila pec!“
(she) did not melt (the) furnace
she did not heat

Nevěsty si tedy řekly, že to udělají
(The) brides themselves so (they) told that thus will do

stejně	jako	žabka.	Těsto	zadělaly	se
as well	like	(the) frog	(The) dough	(they) made	itself

studenou	vodou	a	nalily	ho	do	studené
(with) cold	water	and	(they) poured	it	into	(the) cold

pece.	Ale	když	viděly,	že	se	těsto	rozteklo,
furnace	But	when	(they) saw	that	itself	(the) dough	spilled

rychle	připravily	nové.	Mouku	tentokrát
quickly	(they) prepared	new	(The) flour	this time

smíchaly	s	teplou	vodou	a	daly	do	vyhřáté
mixed	with	warm	water	and	gave	into	(the) heated
					put in		

pece.	Tak	spěchaly,	že	se	jedné	chléb	připálil
furnace	So	(they) rushed	that	itself	one	bread	burned

a	druhé	zůstal	nedopečený.
and	(the) other	stayed	unfinished

Ráno	přišli	bratři	před	krále	s	chlebem.
Morning	came	(the) brothers	before	(the) king	with	(the) bread

Král	ochutnal	chléb	nejstaršího	syna	a	řekl:
(The) king	tasted	(the) bread	(of the) oldest	son	and	said

„Tenhle chléb je takový, že by se dal jíst
This bread is such that would oneself gave to eat

jen z nouze.“ Pak ochutnal chléb
only from in an emergency Then (he) tasted (the) bread

prostředního bratra a povídá: „Ani tenhle chléb
(of the) middle brother and (he) says Neither this bread

není o moc lepší.“ Nakonec ochutnal chléb
not is -about- much better Finally (he) tasted bread

od Ivana, podíval se na něj a řekl: „Tenhle
from Ivan looked himself at him and said This

chléb je nejlepší, budu ho dávat na stůl, až budu
bread is (the) best (I) will it give at table when (I) will

mít hosty.“
have guests

„Vaše ženy splnily všechny mé úkoly,“ řekl potom
Your women fulfilled all my tasks said then

král synům, „a proto vás zítra všechny
(the) king (to the) sons and therefore you tomorrow all

zvu k sobě na hostinu. Ať přijdou i
(I) invite to myself for (a) banquet Let (that) (they) will come also

vaše ženy."
your wives

Ivan z toho měl těžkou hlavu. „Jak já tam s
Ivan from this had (a) heavy head How I there with

sebou přivedu žabku?" říkal si. Žabka ho
myself will bring (the) frog (he) said (to) himself (The) frog him

ale uklidňovala: „Kvak, kvak! Proč si děláš
however reassured Quack quack Why yourself (you) do

starosti, bohatýre Ivane?"
worry hero Ivan

„Otec chce, abych tě zítra přivedl s sebou,"
Father wants so that you tomorrow (I) brought with myself

odpověděl jí smutně.
(he) answered her sadly

„Neměj obavy," usmála se žabka, „ráno
Don't have concerns smiled herself (the) frog tomorrow

bývá	moudřejší	večera.“
is usually	wiser	(in the) evening

Druhý	den	se	Ivan	vydal	k	otci	a
(The) other	day	himself	Ivan	gave out	to	(the) father	and
The next				directed			

nevěsty	starších	bratrů	opět	poslaly	služku,
(the) brides	(of the) elder	brothers	again	sent	(the) maid

aby	zjistila,	jak	žabka	přijede.	Žabka
in order that	(she) found out	how	(the) frog	will arrive	(The) frog

otevřela	okno	a	zavolala	silným	hlasem:
opened	(the) window	and	called	(with a) strong	voice

„Silní	větrové,	leťte	do	mé	říše	a	přiveďte
Strong	wind	fly	to	my	empire	and	bring

kočár	se	vší	nádherou,	se	sluhy,	s
(the) carriage	with	all	(the) splendor	with	(the) servants	with

kočím!“
(the) coachman

Bratři	a	jejich	manželky	už	byli	u	krále,
(The) brothers	and	their	wives	already	were	at	(the) king

když v tom uslyšeli dusot a hluk. Přijížděli
when in this (they) heard clatter and noise Arrived

kočí, za nimi sluhové a nádherný
(the) coachmen behind them (the) servants and (a) wonderful

kočár. Král si pomyslel, že k němu dorazil
carriage (The) king himself thought that to him arrived

nějaký cizí král. „Otče, nikam nechoďte, to je
some foreign king Father nowhere don't go this is

moje žena," řekl Ivan.
my wife said Ivan

Kočár se zastavil, dveře se otevřely
(The) carriage itself stopped (the) doors themselves opened

a ven vystoupila Ivanova žena. Byla tak krásná,
and out stepped Ivan's wife (She) was so beautiful

že všichni v úžasu zůstali stát. Když si
that everyone in awe stayed stand When herself

sedla ke stolu, nevěsty starších bratrů
(she) seated at (the) table (the) brides elder (of the) brothers

se začaly cítit nejistě. Ivanova žena
themselves (they) started to feel uncertain Ivan's wife

vypila část vína a zbytek vylila do
drank part (of the) wine and (the) rest (she) poured into

jednoho rukávu. Kosti z jídla dala do druhého
one sleeve Bones from food (she) put into (the) other

rukávu. Ostatní nevěsty ji začaly napodobovat a
sleeve (The) other brides her started to imitate and

udělaly totéž.
(they) did (the) same

Když skončila hostina, začala hrát hudba a
When ended (the) banquet started to play music and

Ivanova žena šla tancovat. Mávla jedním
Ivan's wife went to dance (She) waved one

rukávem a kolem stolu se objevil potok.
sleeve and around (the) table itself appeared (a) stream

Mávla druhým a po vodě začaly plout
(She) waved (the) other and on (the) water started to swim

husy a labutě. Všichni jen žasli nad její
geese and swans Everyone only admired over her

dovedností. Jakmile ale přestala tančit,
skills As soon as however (she) stopped to dance

všechno zmizelo.
all disappeared

Pak šly tančit ostatní nevěsty. Když mávly
Then went to dance (the) other brides When (they) waved

rukávy, všechny kolem sebe pocákaly vodou
(the) sleeves all around themselves splashed water

a kosti létaly vzduchem, až málem hostům
and bones flew (in the) air then almost (the the) guests

vypíchly oko.
poked out (the) eyes

Po hostině se Ivan rozhodl zničit žabí
On (the) feast himself Ivan decided to destroy (the) frog

kůži, aby jeho žena už zůstala navždy ve
skin in order that his wife already remained forever in

své lidské podobě. Hned, jak dorazil domů,
her human form Now as (he) arrived home

vzal žabí kůži a spálil ji. Za chvíli se
(he) took (the) frog skin and burned her After (a) while herself

objevila jeho žena a hledala kůži. Když ji
appeared his wife and searched (the) skin When her

nenašla, řekla: „Ach, bohatýre Ivane! Když jsi
not found (she) said Ah hero Ivan When (you) are

spálil mou žabí kůži, musíš mě teď hledat.
burned me (the) frog skin (you) must me now search

Najdeš mě daleko odsud, za devatero horami
Find me far from here behind (the) nine mountains

a řekami, v království pod sluncem. Jmenuji
and rivers in (the) kingdom under (the) sun My name is

se Vasilka Přemoudrá."
itself Vasilka Premudra Overwise

Jak to dořekla, zmizela. Ivan si
As this (she) finished saying (she) disappeared Ivan himself

smutně povzdechl, ale rozhodl se, že ji
sadly (he) sighed but decided himself that her

musí najít. Prošel mnoho zemí, lesů a
(he) must find (He) passed many countries forests and

řek. Nakonec dorazil k malé chaloupce, která
rivers Finally (he) arrived to (a) small cottage which

stála na kuřích nožkách a sama se otáčela.
stood on chicken feet and self itself turned

„Chaloupko, chaloupko, otoč se ke mně
Cottage cottage turn yourself to to me

předkem!“ zavolal Ivan. Chaloupka poslechla a
(with the) front called Ivan (The) cottage listened and

Ivan vstoupil. Uvnitř viděl starou Babu Jagu, která
Ivan entered Inside (he) saw (an) old Baba Yaga who

se na něj přísně zadívala a pravila: „Co tu
herself at him severely looked and spoke What here

pohledáváš, bohatýre Ivane?“
(you) are looking for hero Ivan

Ivan jí vypověděl svůj příběh a Baba Jaga se
Ivan her told his story and Baba Yaga herself

zamyslela. „Pomůžu ti," řekla nakonec, „každý
thought I'll help you (she) said finally each

den sem tvoje žena Vasilka přichází odpočívat.
day here your wife Vasilka comes to rest

Když přijde, chyť ji pevně za hlavu, ale
When (she) comes grab her firmly by (the) head but
the hair

nepouštěj ji, ať se promění v cokoliv."
don't let her let herself turns in anything

Jak řekla, tak se stalo. Když Vasilka přišla,
How (she) said so itself happened When Vasilka came

Ivan ji pevně chytil. Začala se měnit –
Ivan her firmly grabbed (She) started herself change –

jednou v hada, potom v ropuchu a nakonec ve
once in (a) snake then in (a) toad and finally in

střelu. Ivan měl strach, ale nakonec střelu
(a) projectile Ivan had fear but finally (the) projectile
a magical bolt the magical bolt

zlomil vejpůl. Hned se před ním objevila jeho
broke in half Now herself before him appeared his

milovaná Vasilka v lidské podobě.
beloved Vasilka in human form

„Teď už jsem navždy tvoje, Ivane," řekla s
Now already (I) am forever yours Ivan (she) said with

úsměvem.
(a) smile

Baba Jaga jim ještě darovala kouzelný létající
Baba Yaga them still donated (a) magical flying

koberec. Ivan a Vasilka se na něj posadili
carpet Ivan and Vasilka themselves on it planted

a za tři dny doletěli zpět k Ivanovu otci.
and for three days (they) flew back to Ivan's father

Král byl šťastný, že se Ivan vrátil se
(The) king was happy that himself Ivan returned with

svou krásnou ženou. Uspořádal velkou hostinu na
his beautiful wife (He) arranged (a) great banquet in

jejich	počest	a	nakonec	jmenoval	Ivana	svým
their	honor	and	finally	named	Ivan	his

nástupcem.
successor

A	tak	bohatýr	Ivan	a	Vasilka	Přemoudrá	žili
And	so	(the) hero	Ivan	and	Vasilka	Premudra (the Superwise)	lived

spolu	šťastně,	vládli	moudře	a	všichni	je	měli
together	happily	ruled	wisely	and	everyone	them	had liked

rádi.
gladly

O hloupém Peciválovi

About the Stupid Pecival

Byl	jednou	jeden	stařík,	který	měl	tři	syny.
(There) was	once	one	old man	who	had	three	sons

Dva	z	nich	byli	rozumní,	ženatí	a	pracovití.
Two	of	them	were	sensible	married	and	hardworking

Třetí	syn,	Pecivál,	byl	naopak	hloupý,	líný
(The) third	son	Pecival	was	on the contrary	stupid	lazy

a	nezadaný.	Když	stařík	cítil,	že	jeho	čas	na
and	single	When	(the) old man	felt	that	his	time	on

tomto	světě	končí,	rozdělil	svůj	majetek
this	world	ends was ending	(he) distributed	his	property

mezi	dva	starší	syny	a	každému	ze
between	(the) two	older	sons	and	(to) every one	from

tří	bratrů	dal	po	stu	zlatých.	Brzy
(the) three	brothers	gave	-on-	(a) hundred	gold (pieces)	Soon

nato zemřel.
thereafter (he) died

Po pohřbu začali starší bratři hospodařit, ale
After (the) funeral started (the) older brothers to farm but

Pecivál zůstal takový, jaký byl – líný a málo
Pecival stayed such how (he) was - lazy and little

pracovitý. Jednoho dne přišli bratři za
hardworking One day came (the) brothers for

Pecivále m a řekli:
Pecival and (they) said

„Poslouchej, Peciv ále. Dej nám své peníze. My
Listen Pecival Give us your money We

pojedeme do světa za výdělkem a až
will go into (the) world for earnings and when

se vrátíme, přivezeme ti červenou
ourselves (we) will return (we) will deliver you (a) red

čepici, červený pás a červené boty. Mezitím
hat (a) red belt and red shoes Meanwhile

budeš doma poslouchat naše ženy.“
(you) will (at) home listen to our women

Pecivál si odjakživa přál červenou čepici, pás
Pecival himself from always wished (a) red hat belt

i boty, a tak nadšeně souhlasil a dal jim
and shoes and so enthusiastically agreed and gave them

všechny své peníze. Bratři odešli a Pecivál
all his money (The) brothers left and Pecival

zůstal doma. Celé dny jen ležel na peci,
stayed (at) home (The) whole day only lay on (the) furnace

a když mu švagrové něco poručily,
and when him (the) sisters-in-law something asked

odmítal je poslouchat. Zato mu nade vše
(he) refused them to listen to But him from all

chutnaly cibule, zaprážky a kvas.
tasted (best) onions rusks and kvass

Jednoho dne na něj švagrové zavolaly:
One day on him (the) sisters-in-law (they) called

„Peciválе, zajdi pro vodu!“
Pecival go for water

Byla zima a venku mrzlo, takže se mu z
(It) was winter and outside frosty so himself him from

pece nechtělo. „Jděte si samy,“
(the) furnace unwillingly Go yourself selves
he didn't want to go

odsekl.
(he) answered

Švagrové ho ale přemlouvaly: „Jdi,
(The) sisters-in-law him however coaxed Go

Peciválе, my ti zatím připravíme cibuli,
Pecival we you meanwhile prepare onions

zaprážky a kvas. A jestli neposlechneš, až
rusks and kvass And if (you) won't listen when

se vrátí tvoji bratři, nedostaneš ani čepici,
themselves return your brothers (you) won't get neither hat

ani pás, ani boty!“
nor belt nor shoes

To Pecivála přesvědčilo. Neochotně slezl z
This Pecival convinced Reluctantly (he) went from

pece, vzal konve a sekeru a šel k řece.
(the) furnace took (a) can and axe and went to (the) river

Když dorazil, vysekal díru do ledu, nabral
When (he) arrived (he) cut out (a) hole in (the) ice scooped up

vodu a položil konve na led. Jak tak stál
water and placed (the) can on (the) ice As so (he) stood

a koukal do vody, uviděl štiku. Rychle ji
and looked at (the) water (he) saw (a) pike Quickly her

chytil.
(he) grabbed

„Pusť mě!“ prosila štika. „A já ti za to splním,
Let go me begged (the) pike And I you for this will grant

co si budeš přát.“
what yourself (you) will wish

Pecivál chvíli přemýšlel a pak řekl: „Chci mít
Pecival (a) while thought and then said (I) want to have

dar, aby se všechno, co řeknu, hned
more in order that itself all what (I) say (is) now

splnilo."
fulfilled

Štika odpověděla: „Dobře, jen vyslov slova:
(The) pike answered Good only pronounce (the) words

Na mé úsilné žádání,
On my effortful request

a na štičí rozkázání,
and on pike's command

ať se stane to a to!"
let itself happens this and this

Pecivál to vyzkoušel:
Pecival this tried

„Na mé úsilné žádání,
On my effortful request

a na štičí rozkázání,
and on pike's command

ať je tu cibule, kvas a zaprážky!“
let is here onions kvass and rusks

V tu chvíli se před ním všechno objevilo. Najedl
In here time itself before him all appeared (He) fed

se, napil a spokojeně řekl: „Dobře, tohle
himself (he) drank and satisfied (he) said Good this

funguje.“ Pak pustil štiku zpátky do vody.
works Then (he) let (the) pike back into (the) waters

Před návratem k domovu zkusil ještě jednou:
Before returning to home (he) tried still once

„Na mé úsilné žádání,
On my effortful request

a na štičí rozkázání,
and on pike's command

ať jsou ty konve doma!“
let are you cans (at) home

Konve se zvedly a samy vyrazily
(The) cans themselves picked up and themselves set off

směrem	k	chalupě,	zatímco	Pecivál	šel	za
towards	to	(the) cottage	while	Pecival	(he) went	after

nimi,	spokojeně	si	žvýkal	cibuli	a	zapíjel
them	satisfied	himself	chewed	onions	and	drank washed down

ji	kvasem.	Když	konve	dorazily	domů,	Pecivál
them	(with) kvass	When	(the) cans	arrived	home	Pecival

si	zase	vylezl	na	pec	a	usnul.
himself	again	climbed out	on	(the) furnace	and	fell asleep

Za	pár	dní	ho	švagrové	znovu
After	(a) couple	(of) days	him	(the) sisters-in-law	again

vyrušily:
interrupted

„Pecivále,	naštípej	nám	dříví!“
Pecival	split	us	(some) firewood

„Proč	si	ho	nenaštípete	samy?“	bručel
Why	yourself	him	(you) won't find	(it) self	grumbled

Pecivál.
Pecival

„Protože to má dělat muž! Jestli dříví
Because this has to do (a) man If firewood

nenaštípeš, necháme tě na peci zmrznout
(you) won't chop (we)'ll leave you on (the) furnace freeze

a nedostaneš žádné boty ani čepici!“
and (you) won't get any shoes nor hat

Pecivál zamumlal kouzelnou formulku:
Pecival muttered (the) magic formula

„Na mé úsilné žádání,
On my effortful request

a na štičí rozkázání,
and on pike's command

ať se hned stane, co chtějí!“
let itself now happen what (they) want

Sekyra sama vyskočila zpod lavice, nasekala
(The) axe itself popped up from (the) bench chopped

dřevo a nanosila ho ke kamnům. Pecivál
(the) wood and carried it to (the) stove Pecival

zatím ležel na peci, jedl zaprážky a
meanwhile lay on (the) furnace ate rusks and

zapíjel je kvasem.
drank them (with) kvass
washed down

Za pár dní se švagrové ozvaly
After (a) couple (of) days themselves (the) sisters-in-law said

znovu:
again

„Pecivále, v dřevníku už není žádné dřevo.
Pecival in (the) woodshed already not is any wood

Jeď do lesa a přivez nové!“
Go to (the) forest and bring new

Tentokrát Pecivál poslechl. Oblékl se, vzal
This time Pecival listened (He) dressed himself took

sáně, naložil na ně trochu cibule a zaprážek a
(a) sled loaded on it a little onion and rusks and

řekl:
said

„Na mé úsilné žádání,
On my effortful request

a na štičí rozkázání,
and on pike's command

ať ty sáně jedou samy do lesa!“
let you sled go yourself to (the) forest

Sáně se samy rozjely. Po cestě projížděl
(The) sled itself slef started On (the) road passed

Pecivál městem a způsobil pořádný rozruch.
Pecival (through a) town and caused (a) proper stir

Lidé vybíhali z domů, aby se
People ran out from (the) house in order that themselves

podívali, jak sáně jedou bez koní. Při své
(they) see how (a) sled comes without horses At his

cestě ale porazil několik vozů a polekal
(the) road however (he) beat several wagons and scared

ženy i děti.
women and children

Když dojel do lesa, řekl:
When (he) arrived to (the) forest (he) said

„Na mé úsilné žádání,
On my effortful request

a na štičí rozkázání,
and on pike's command

ať se naseká dříví, uváže do otýpek a naloží
let itself chop firewood tie (it) into bundles and load (it)

na sáně!“
on (the) sled

Všechno se stalo tak, jak řekl. Když měl
All itself happened so as (he) said When (he) had

dřevo naložené, vydal se zpět. Jenže ve
(fire)wood loaded gave out himself back But in
he directed

městě si na něj lidé počíhali. Jakmile ho
(the) town themselves for him people waited As soon as him

spatřili, strhli ho ze saní a začali
(they) spotted (they) ripped off him from (the) sled and started

ho bít.
him to hit

Pecivál se zpočátku smál, myslel si, že
Pecival himself initially laughed (he) thought himself that

ho chtějí polechtat. Ale když rány začaly
him (they) want to tickle But when (the) wounds started

bolet, zamračil se a vykřikl:
to hurt (he) frowned himself and (he) exclaimed

„Na mé úsilné žádání,
On my effortful request

a na štičí rozkázání,
and on pike's command

ať všichni dostanou polenem!“
let everyone get (with a) log

Polena ze saní vyskočila a začala skákat po
Logs from (the) sled popped up and started to jump on

lidech, až se všichni rozprchli na všechny
(the) people then themselves everyone dispersed to all

strany. Pecivál se smál na celé kolo a
directions Pecival himself laughed on (a) full round and

spokojeně se vrátil domů, kde si zase
satisfied himself returned home where himself again

vylezl na svou pec.
(he) climbed back on his stove

Po celém kraji se začalo mluvit o
On throughout (the) counties itself started talk about

Peciválovi a jeho zázracích. Lidé se na něj
Pecival and his miracles People themselves at him

chodili dívat, jako by byl divotvůrce. Brzy
(they) went to watch as would was (a) miracle worker Soon

se o něm doslechl i samotný král. Chtěl
himself about him heard also (the) very king Wanted

ho poznat, a tak pro něj nechal poslat svého
him to get to know and so for him let send his

vojevůdce.
general

„Slez z pece, Pecivále! Ustroj se a
Get down from (the) stove Pecival Dress yourself and

pojď ke králi!“ přikázal vojevůdce.
go to (to the) king ordered (the) general

Pecivál líně odpověděl: „Proč? Však mám doma
Pecival lazily answered Why However (I) have (at) home

dost cibule, kvasu a zaprážek.“
enough onions kvass and rusks

Vojevůdce se rozzlobil a uštědřil Peciválovi
(The) general himself angered and granted Pecival

pohlavek. Ale Pecivál jen klidně zamumlal:
(a) slap But Pecival only calmly muttered

„Na mé úsilné žádání,
On my effortful request

a na štičí rozkázání,
and on pike's command

ať dostane pometlem!“
let get (it) (with a) broom

Vtom	se	zpoza	kamna	vyřítilo	špinavé
In that	itself	from behind	(the) stove	rushed	(a) dirty

pometlo,	celé	omočené,	a	začalo	vojevůdce	mlátit.
broom	fully	soaked	and	started	(the) general	to beat

Chudák	sotva	utekl	oknem	a	vrátil
(The) poor guy	barely	escaped	(through the) window	and	returned

se	ke	králi	celý	zmazaný	a	bez	úspěchu.
himself	to	(the) king	wholly	smeared	and	without	success
				dirty			

Král	poslal	jiného	posla,	opatrnějšího.	Ten
(The) king	sent	another	messenger	more cautious	This one

si	napřed	zjistil,	co	má	Pecivál	rád.	Když
himself	first	found out	what	has	Pecival	gladly	When

přišel	k	jeho	peci,	poklonil	se	a	mile
(he) came	to	his	furnace	(he) bowed	himself	and	pleasantly

řekl:	„Peciválе,	pojeď	se	mnou	ke	králi!	Chce
said	Pecival	come	with	me	to	(the) king	(He) wants

ti	dát	červenou	čepici,	červený	pás	a	červené
you	give	(a) red	hat	(a) red	belt	and	red
to give you							

boty.“
shoes

„Jestli je to tak, pojedu. Jeďte napřed, já vás
If is this (is) so (I)'ll go Go in front first I (with) you

dohoním,“ odpověděl Pecivál.
will catch up answered Pecival

Posel odjel, ale Pecivál se nikam nehnal.
(The) messenger left but Pecival himself nowhere not drove

V klidu snědl své zaprážky s cibulí, zapil
In calmness (he) ate his rusks with onions drank down

je kvasem a šel si lehnout. Když ho
them (with) kvass and (he) went himself to lie down When him

bratři vzbudili a připomněli mu cestu
(the) brothers awakened and reminded him (of the) journey

ke králi, Pecivál se jen protáhl na peci
to (the) king Percival himself only stretched on (the) stove

a řekl:
and said

„Na mé úsilné žádání,
On my effortful request

a na štičí rozkázání,
and on pike's command

ať na té peci se objevím hned před
let that on that furnace myself (I)'ll find now before

králem!“
(the) king

Pec se zakouřila, zapálila a dveře
(The) furnace itself smoked lit and (the) doors

se rozletěly. Pec s Peciválem se
themselves (they) flew (The) furnace with Pecival itself

rozjela po silnici, předhonila posla a
started on (the) road overtook (the) messenger and

zastavila se přímo před královským palácem.
stopped itself directly in front of (the) royal palace

Král se svým dvorem vyběhl na pavlač,
(The) king with his court ran on porch

aby se na tu podivnou scénu podíval.
in order that themselves at this weird scene looked

Pecivál na peci dojídal zaprážky a
Pecival on (the) furnace finished eating rusks and

zapíjel je kvasem, nikoho si nevšímal.
drank them (with) kvass no-one himself not noticed

„Kdo jsi, co tu děláš a proč jsi
Who are (you) what here (you) do and why (you) are

přijel?“ ptal se král.
arrived asked himself (the) king

„Jsem Pecivál. Jím zaprážky s cibulí a piju
(I) am Pecival (I) eat rusks with onions and (I) drink

kvas. Přijel jsem si pro červenou čepici,
kvass Arrived (I) am myself for (a) red hat

červený pás a červené boty,“ odpověděl Pecivál.
(a) red belt and red shoes answered Pecival

Během rozhovoru se na pavlač přišla
During (the) conversation herself on (the) pavilion came

podívat králova dcera. Byla tak krásná, že
to see (the) king's daughter (She) was so beautiful that

se do ní Pecivál hned zamiloval. V duchu
himself to (of) her Pecival now loved In spirit
his mind

si přál:
himself (he) wished

„Na mé úsilné žádání,
On my effortful request

a na štičí rozkázání,
and on pike's command

ať se královna stane mou milou!“
let herself (the) queen become me dear
fall in love with me

Pec se znovu rozjela a Pecivál odjel
(The) furnace itself again started and Pecival left

domů. Když se pec vrátila na své místo,
(for) home When itself (the) furnace returned on its place

Pecivál si na ni zase lehl, jedl cibuli se
Pecival himself on her again lay down ate onions with

zaprážkami a byl spokojený.
rusks and was satisfied

Mezitím se však králova dcera zamilovala
Meanwhile herself however (the) king's daughter loved

do Pecivála. Nemohla bez něj být, padla před
to Pecival She couldn't without him be fell before

králem na kolena a vyznala mu pravdu.
(the) king on (the) knees and confessed him (the) truth

Král se jí snažil Pecivála rozmluvit, ale
(The) king himself her tried Pecival to talk out of but

marně. Nakonec poslal pro Pecivála znovu.
in vain Finally (he) sent for Pecival again

Tentokrát ho posel opil, svázal a
This time him (the) messenger (got) drunk bound and

přivezl ke králi.
brought to (the) king

Král byl rozhněvaný. Zavolal černokněžníka, dal
(The) king was angry (He) called (a) sorcerer gave

Peciválа i s princeznou zavřít do skleněného
Pecival and with (the) princess locked into (a) glass

sudu, zasmolit ho a vyhodil do povětří. Sud
barrel tarred it and blew into (the) air (The) barrel

letěl vysoko nad zemí, jako by byl pták.
flew high over (the) earth as would was (a) bird

Princezna v sudě plakala a prosila Peciválа,
(The) princess in (the) barrel cried and begged Pecival

aby ji zachránil. Pecivál se nejdřív tvářil
in order that her (he) saved Pecival himself first looked

lhostejně: „V sudě je mi dobře." Nakonec ho
indifferently In (the) barrel is to me good Finally him
I'm fine

však princezniny prosby obměkčily. Vyslovil:
however (the) princess' pleas softened (He) spoke

„Na mé úsilné žádání,
On my effortful request

a na štičí rozkázání,
and on pike's command

ať se hned octnu na pustém ostrově!“
let ourselves now find on (an) empty island

Sud se zastavil nad mořem, snesl se na
(The) barrel itself stopped over (the) sea bore down itself on

ostrov a rozpadl se. Pecivál a princezna byli
(an) island and fell apart itself Pecival and (the) princess were

volní. Ostrov byl kouzelný – stačilo si
free (The) island was magical – enough oneself

něco přát a všeho bylo dost. Měli co
something to wish and all was enough Had something

jíst, co pít a všechno se samo
to eat something drink and all itself only

objevovalo a zase mizelo. Pecivál byl nadšený,
appeared and again disappeared Pecival was enthusiastic

ale princezna chtěla víc. Prosila Peciválа,
but (the) princess wanted more (She) begged Pecival

aby jí nechal postavit palác.
in order that her let build (a) palace

„Na mé úsilné žádání,
On my effortful request

a na štičí rozkázání,
and on pike's command

ať tu stojí nádherný palác!“
let here stand (a) wonderful palace

Palác byl rázem hotový. Byl z mramoru, s
Palace was at once finished (It) was from marble with

okny z křišťálu, zlatým nábytkem a
windows from crystal (with) gold furniture and

jantarovou střechou. Princezna ale pořád
amber roof (The) princess however still

nebyla spokojená. Chtěla, aby byl ostrov
was not satisfied (She) wanted in order that was (the) island

spojený s pevninou a aby na ostrov
linked to with (the) mainland for in order that on (the) island

přišli lidé. Také si přála vidět svého otce.
came people Also herself wished to see his father

Pecivál tedy řekl:
Pecival thus said

„Na mé úsilné žádání,
On my effortful request

a na štičí rozkázání,
and on pike's command

ať se stane, co si princezna přeje!“
let itself happen what herself (the) princess wishes

Druhý den stál přes moře křišťálový most se
(The) other day stood over (the) sea (a) crystal bridge with
The next

zlatými oblouky a diamantovým zábradlím. Pecivál
golden arches and diamond railing Pecival

a královna se vydali po mostě k
and (the) queen themselves gave out on (the) bridge to
went out

paláci krále.
(the) palace (of the) king

Před cestou si však Pecivál uvědomil, že
Before (the) way himself however Pecival realized that

jako hlupák by se na královském dvoře
as fool would himself in (the) royal court

zesměšnil. Rozhodl se použít kouzlo
mocked (He) decided himself to use (the) magic

naposledy:
last

„Na mé úsilné žádání,
On my effortful request

a na štičí rozkázání,
and on pike's command

ať se hned stanu rozumným!“
let myself now become reasonable

V tu chvíli nabyl rozumu a slušnosti. S
In this moment (he) regained reason and decency With

princeznou se vydali ke králi. Když
(the) princess themselves (they) gave out they went out to (the) king When

dorazili, padli králi k nohám a prosili o
(they) arrived (they) fell (the) king to (the) feet and asked for

požehnání. Král nakonec dal své svolení a
blessings (The) king finally gave his permission and

Pecivál se oženil s princeznou.
Pecival himself married with (the) princess

Po svatbě král jmenoval Peciválа svým
On (the) wedding (the) king named Pecival his

nástupcem. Na oslavu uspořádali slavnostní
successor For celebration (they) arranged (a) ceremonial

hody, kde se jedlo, pilo a veselilo, až
feast where itself (was) food drink and cheer then

se o tom vyprávělo po celé zemi.
itself about this told in (the) whole country

Tři zlaté vlasy děda Vševěda
Three Golden Hairs of Grandfather Vsheved

Byl	jednou	jeden	král,	který	rád	lovil	v
(There) was	once	one	king	who	gladly	hunted	in

lese.	Jednoho	dne	pronásledoval	jelena	tak
(the) forest	One	day	(he) hunted	(a) deer	so

dlouho,	až	zabloudil.	Byl	sám,	blížila	se
long	until	(he) got lost	(He) was	by himself	approached	itself

noc,	a	tak	byl	rád,	když	našel	na	mýtině
night	and	so	(he) was	happy	when	(he) found	in	(a) clearing

chalupu.	Uvnitř	bydlel	uhlíř.
(a) cottage	Inside	lived	(a) charcoal maker

„Uhlíři,“	řekl	král,	„vyveď	mě	z	lesa,
Charcoal maker	said	(the) king	bring out	me	from out of	(the) forest,

dobře	ti	zaplatím.“
good well	you	(I)'ll pay

Uhlíř odpověděl: „Rád bych, ale žena
(The) charcoal maker answered Gladly (I) would but (the) wife

mi právě rodí. Nemohu teď odejít. Zůstaňte
me just gave birth (I) can't now leave Stay
of mine

přes noc tady, lehněte si na půdu,
over night here lie down yourself on (the) ground

ráno vás dovedu na cestu.“
(in the) morning you (I) lead to on (the) road
I will guide to

Král si lehl na půdu, ale nemohl
(The) king himself lay down on (the) ground but couldn't

usnout. O půlnoci viděl světlo přicházející ze
fall asleep About midnight (he) saw light incoming from

světnice. Podíval se škvírou ve
(the) living room (He) looked himself through (a) crack in

stropě a uviděl tři bílé babičky se svícemi.
(the) ceiling and (he) saw three white old ladies with candles
the floor

Byly to Sudičky.
Were these Judges
These were the weird sisters

První řekla: „Tomu chlapci dávám, aby
First said To this boy (I) give in order that
The first one (baby)

zažil velká nebezpečí.“
(he) experienced (a) great danger
he shall experience

Druhá řekla: „A já mu dávám, aby vždy
Other said And I him give in order that always
The second he always

šťastně vyvázl.“
happily out-stucks
gets out

Třetí dodala: „A já mu dávám za ženu dceru
Third added And I him give for wife (the) daughter
The third

toho krále, který tu nahoře leží na seně.“
of this king who here above lies on (the) hay

Pak Sudičky zmizely.
Then (the) Judges disappeared
the weird sisters

Král zůstal jako zkamenělý. Celou noc
(The) king stayed as petrified (The) entire night

přemýšlel, jak zabránit tomu, co slyšel.
(he) thought how to avoid this what (he) heard

Ráno, když dítě zaplakalo, uhlíř
(In the) morning when (the) child cried (the) charcoal maker

zjistil, že jeho žena zemřela.
found that his wife (had) died

„Och, můj sirotečku, co si teď počnu?“ plakal
Oh my little orphan what myself now (I) do cried

uhlíř.
(the) charcoal maker

„Dej mi to dítě,“ řekl král, „postarám se o
Give me this child said (the) king (I) will take care myself of

něj. A tobě dám tolik peněz, že už
him And to you (I) will give so much money that already

nikdy nebudeš muset pálit uhlí.“
never (you) won't have to burn charcoal

Uhlíř souhlasil a král slíbil, že
(The) charcoal maker agreed and (the) king promised that

si pro dítě pošle. Když se
himself for (the) child sends When himself
he will let someone come

vrátil do svého zámku, dozvěděl se, že
(he) returned to his castle (he) found out himself that

se mu narodila dcera – právě té noci, kdy
itself him (was) born (a) daughter – just that night when

viděl Sudičky. Král si vzpomněl na
(he) saw the Judges (The) king himself remembered on
the three weird sisters

jejich slova, zamračil se a přemýšlel, jak se
their words frowned himself and thought how himself

dítěte zbavit.
(from the) child to get rid of

Zavolal si sluhu: „Půjdeš k uhlíři,
(He) called himself (a) servant (You) go to (the) charcoal maker

vezmeš to dítě a utopíš ho v řece. Jinak
take that child and drown him in (the) river Otherwise

si to odskáčeš!“
yourself this you'll pay for it!

Sluha šel, vzal dítě v košíku a hodil ho
(The) servant went took (the) child in (a) basket and threw him

do hluboké řeky. „Dobrou noc, nezvaný zeti,“
into (the) deep river Good night uninvited son-in-law

pomyslel si král.
thought himself (the) king

Ale dítě se neutopilo. Košík plul po
But (the) child himself not-drowned (The) basket floated on

řece, až doplul k chalupě rybáře.
(the) river then sailed to (the) cottage (of a) fisherman

Rybář zrovna opravoval sítě, když zahlédl
(The) fisherman just repaired nets when (he) spotted
was just repairing

košík. Vytáhl ho z vody a našel
(the) basket (He) got out it from (the) water and (he) found

uvnitř dítě.
inside (a) child

„Ženo, vždycky sis přála syna. Tady je –
Wife always ourselves (we) wished (a) son Here (it) is -

přinesla ho voda,“ řekl rybář.
brought along him (the) water said (the) fisherman

Žena byla šťastná a dítě si zamilovala.
(The) woman was happy and (the) child herself loved

Pojmenovali ho Plaváček, protože připlaval po
Named him Floater because (he) swam on

vodě.
(the) water

Čas plynul a z Plaváčka vyrostl krásný
Time flowed and from Floater grew up (a) handsome

mládenec, jakého široko daleko nebylo.
bachelor of which wide (and) far not was (an equal)

Jednou v létě přijel k rybáři král. Bylo
Once in summer arrived to (the) fisherman (the) king (It) was

horko, chtěl se napít a požádal o
hot (he) wanted himself drink and requested by about

vodu. Když mu Plaváček podal čistou vodu,
water When him Floater gave over handed clean water

král si ho prohlédl a zarazil se.
(the) king himself him viewed and stopped himself

„Šikovného chlapce máš, rybáři," řekl. „Je to
(A) clever boy (you) have fisherman (he) said Is this

tvůj syn?"
your son

„Ano i ne," odpověděl rybář. „Před dvaceti
Yes and no answered (the) fisherman Before (of) twenty

lety připlaval po řece v košíku a
years (he) floated on (the) river in (a) basket and

vychovali jsme ho."
raised (we) are him
we have raised him

Král zbledl. Poznal, že je to dítě, které
(The) king paled (He) knew that is this (the) child who

měl být utopeno.
(he) had be drowned
he let

Hned se však vzpamatoval a řekl: „Potřebuji
Now himself however (he) recovered and said (I) need

posla. Může mi ten chlapec doručit psaní do
(a) messenger Can me this boy delivered (a) letter to

mého zámku?“
my castle

„Samozřejmě,“ odpověděl rybář.
Of course answered (the) fisherman

Král napsal dopis své ženě:
(The) king wrote (a) letter (to) his wife

„Toho mladíka, kterého ti posílám, dej bez
This young man who you (I) send let without

odkladu popravit. Je to můj nepřítel. Až se
delay execute Is this my enemy When myself
This is

vrátím, ať je vykonáno. Taková je má vůle.“
(I) return let that (it) is carried out Such is my will

Dopis zapečetil a dal ho Plaváčkovi.
(The) letter (he) sealed and gave it (to) Floater

Plaváček se vydal na cestu, ale v lese
Floater himself gave out on (the) road but in (the) forest
directed

zabloudil. Bloudil dlouho, až potkal starou
(he) strayed (He) wandered long then (he) met (an) old

babičku.
grandmother

„Kam míříš, Plaváčku?“ zeptala se.
Where are (you) heading to Floater (she) asked -herself-

„Nesu dopis do královského zámku, ale ztratil
(I) carry (a) letter to (the) royal castle but (I) lost

se po cestě,“ odpověděl.
myself on (the) road (he) answered

„Zůstaň u mě přes noc,“ řekla babička. „Jsem
Stay with me over night said (the) grandma (I) am

tvoje kmotra.“
your godmother

Plaváček přijal její pozvání. Když usnul,
Floater accepted her invitation When (he) fell asleep

babička otevřela jeho kapsu, vzala dopis a
(the) old woman opened his pocket took (the) letter and

vyměnila ho za jiný.
replaced it by another

V novém dopise stálo:
In (the) new letter stood

„Toho mladíka, kterého ti posílám, dej ihned
This young man who you (I) send let immediately

oddat s naší dcerou. Je to můj vyvolený
give away with our daughter Is this my chosen
marry

zeť. Až se vrátím, ať je
son-in-law When myself (I) will return let that (this) is

vykonáno. Taková je má vůle.“
carried out Such is my will

–
–

Když královna přečetla dopis, svolala
When (the) queen read (the) letter (she) convened

ihned svatbu. Nový ženich, Plaváček,
immediately (the) wedding (The) new groom Floater

se všem líbil, a mladá princezna byla
himself to all liked and (the) young princess was

šťastná. Plaváček si svou královskou nevěstu
happy Floater himself his royal bride

také oblíbil. Po několika dnech se vrátil
also liked After several days himself returned

král. Když viděl, co se stalo, rozzlobil
(the) king When (he) saw what itself stood (he) angered
had happened

se.
himself

„Co jsi to udělala?“ křičel na královnu.
What (you) are this done for (he) shouted at (the) queen
have you

„Ale vždyť jsi mi to sám poručil,“
But after all (you) are me this yourself commanded
you have

odpověděla klidně a ukázala mu dopis.
(she) answered calmly and (she) showed him (the) letter

Král si dopis prohlédl. Písmo, pečeť i
(The) king himself (the) letter viewed Font seal and

papír – všechno bylo jeho. Zavolal si Plaváčka
paper – all was his Called himself Floater

a začal ho vyslýchat.
and started him to interrogate

„Kde jsi vzal to psaní?“
Where (you) are took this letter
did you take

Plaváček popsal, jak šel lesem,
Floater described how (he) went (through the) forest

zabloudil a zůstal přes noc u staré babičky,
strayed and stayed over night at (an) old grandmother

která ho zachránila.
who him saved
kept safe

Král poznal, že to byla stejná Sudička, která
(The) king knew that this was (the) same Judge who
weird sister

před lety přisoudila jeho dceru uhlířovu
before years attributed his daughter (the) charcoal maker's
years ago destined

synovi. Zatímco přemýšlel, jak se nechtěného
son While (he) thought how himself (the) unwanted

zetě zbavit, řekl:
son-in-law to get rid of (he) said

„Dobře, co se stalo, to nezměníme. Ale
Good what itself happened this (we) will not change But

nemůžeš si mou dceru vzít jen tak.
(you) can't yourself my daughter take just like that

Přineseš mi tři zlaté vlasy Děda-Vševěda. To
Bring me three golden hairs (from) Grandpa-Vsheved This
from Grandpa All-Knowing

bude její věno."
will be her dowry

Plaváček se rozloučil se svou milou a
Floater himself said farewell from his beloved and

vydal se na cestu. Šel dlouho a
gave out himself on (the) journey (He) went long and
directed

daleko, až dorazil k černému moři. Na břehu
far then (he) arrived at (the) black sea On (the) shore

viděl loď a starého přívozníka.
(he) saw (a) boat and (an) old ferryman

„Pozdrav pánbůh, přívozníku!" zavolal.
Get well (the) lord ferryman (he) called out
May bless you

„Dejž to pánbůh, mladý poutníku! Kam máš
Grant this lord (this) young pilgrim Where (you) have
are you

namířeno?“
directed
going

„Jdu k dědu Vševědu pro tři zlaté vlasy.“
I go to grandpa Vsheved for three (a) golden hairs
(all-knowing)

„Už dlouho tady čekám na takového posla,“
Already long here (I) wait on such (a) messenger

řekl přívozník. „Už dvacet let převážím
said (the) ferryman Already twenty years I'm transporting

lidi sem a tam a nikdo mě nepřichází
people here and there and no one me is not coming

vysvobodit. Zeptáš se děda Vševěda, kdy
to deliver (You) ask yourself grandpa Vsheved when
to redeem All-knowing

bude mé roboty konec?“
will my work end

Plaváček slíbil, že se zeptá, a přívozník
Floater promised that himself (he) asks and (the) ferryman

ho převezl přes moře.
him transported over (the) sea

Pak došel k velikému městu, které vypadalo
Then (he) reached to (a) great city which seemed

opuštěné a smutné. Před bránou potkal
abandoned and sad In front of (the) gate (he) met

starého muže o holi.
(an) old men on (a) stick

„Pozdrav pánbůh, dědečku!“ řekl Plaváček.
Get well (the) lord grandfather said Floater
May bless you

„Dejž to pánbůh, mládenečku! Kam jdeš?“
Grant this one (the) lord young man Where (you) go

„Jdu k dědu Vševědu pro tři zlaté vlasy.“
(I) go to grandpa Vsheved for three golden hairs
All-knowing

„To tě musím odvést k našemu králi,“ řekl
This you (I) have to take away to our (the) king said

stařeček.
(the) old man

Král Plaváčka uvítal a řekl:
(The) king Floater welcomed and said

„Kdysi jsme měli jabloň, která plodila
Once upon a time (we) are had (an) apple tree which grew
we have

zázračná jablka. Kdo snědl jedno jablko, omládl
miraculous apples Who ate one apple got younger

a nabyl nové síly. Ale už dvacet let
and regained new forces But already twenty years

jabloň nerodí. Zeptáš se děda Vševěda,
(the) apple tree not grew (You) ask yourself grandpa Vsheved
All-knowing

proč to tak je?“
why this so is

Plaváček slíbil, že zjistí odpověď, a
Floater promised that (he) finds out (the) answer and

šel dál.
(he) went further

Po dlouhé cestě dorazil do jiného města, které
On (the) long road (he) arrived to another city which

bylo z poloviny zbořené. Nedaleko města viděl
was from halves taken down Near (the) city (he) saw

muže, jak pohřbívá svého otce a při tom pláče.
(a) man how (he) buries his father and at this cries

„Pozdrav pánbůh, smutný hrobníku," řekl Plaváček.
Get well (the) lord sad gravedigger said Floater
May bless you

„Dejž to pánbůh, dobrý poutníku! Kam máš
Grant this one (the) lord good pilgrim Where (you) have
are you

namířeno?"
directions
traveling to

„Jdu k dědu Vševědu pro tři zlaté vlasy."
(I) go to grandpa Vsheved for three golden hairs
All-knowing

„Musím tě zavést k našemu králi. Ten už
(I) must you introduce to our king This one already

dlouho čeká na někoho, kdo by mu pomohl."
long waits for someone who would him helped

Král řekl:
(The) king said

„Kdysi	jsme	měli	studnu	se	živou	vodou.
Once upon a time	(we) are	had	(a) well	with	live	water
	we have					

Kdo	ji	pil,	uzdravil	se,	a	dokonce	i
Who	her	drank	healed	himself	and	even	also

mrtvé	dokázala	oživit.	Ale	už	dvacet	let
(the) dead	(she) proved	to make alive	But	already	twenty	years

je	studna	vyschlá.	Zeptáš	se	děda	Vševěda,
is	(the) well	dried up	(You) ask	yourself	grandpa	Vsheved
						All-knowing

jestli	nám	může	pomoci?“
if	us	(he) can	help

Plaváček	přislíbil,	že	zjistí,	co	se	dá
Floater	promised	that	(he) finds out	what	himself	can

dělat,	a	pokračoval	dál.
do	and	continued	further

Po	dlouhé	a	únavné	cestě	přišel	k	obrovskému
On	(the) long	and	tiresome	road	(he) came	to	(a) huge

lesu.	Uprostřed	lesa	byla	zelená	louka	a
woods	(In the) middle	(of the) forest	was	(a) green	meadow	and

na	ní	stál	zlatý	zámek,	který	se	třpytil
on	(of) her	stood	(a) golden	castle	which	itself	glittered

jako	oheň.	To	byl	zámek	děda	Vševěda.
like	(a) fire	This	was	(the) castle	(of) grandpa	Vsheved
						All-knowing

Plaváček	vešel	dovnitř	a	našel	tam	jen	starou
Floater	went	inside	and	found	there	only	(an) old

babičku,	která	předla	u	kolovrátku.
grandmother	who	spun	at	(a) spinning wheel

„Vítám	tě,	Plaváčku!“	řekla	babička.	Byla	to
Welcome	to you	Floater	said	(the) grandmother	Was	this

jeho	stará	kmotra.	„Co	tě	sem	přivádí?“
his	old	godmother	What	you	here	brought

„Král	nechce,	abych	byl	zadarmo	jeho
(The) king	doesn't want	so that	(I) was	for nothing	his
			I become		

zetěm.	Poslal	mě	pro	tři	zlaté	vlasy	děda
son-in-law	(He) sent	me	for	three	golden	hairs	(of) grandpa

Vševěda.“
Vsheved
All-knowing

Babička se usmála. „Děd Vševěd je můj
(The) old lady herself smiled Grandfather Vsheved All-knowing is my

syn, jasné Slunce. Ráno je malý
son (the) bright Sun (In the) morning (he) is (a) small

chlapec, v poledne muž a večer starý
boy at noon (a) man and (in the) evening (an) old

děda. Neboj se, ty vlasy ti opatřím.
grandfather Don't worry yourself your hairs for your (I) will get

Ale nemůžeš tady zůstat na dohled. Když můj
But (you) can't here stay in surveillance eye shot When my

syn přijde hladový domů, mohl by tě sníst.
son comes hungry home (he) could would you eat

Schovám tě do prázdné kádi."
Hide yourself into (an) empty vat

Plaváček jí poděkoval a poprosil ji, aby
Floater her thanked and asked her in order that

se také děda Vševěda zeptala na otázky,
herself also grandpa Vsheved All-knowing (she) asked for (the) questions

které	slíbil	cestou	zjistit.
which	(he) promised	(on the) road	(to) find out

„Dobře,“	řekla	babička.	„Zeptám	se.	Jen
Good	said	(the) old lady	(I) will ask	myself him	Just

poslouchej,	co	odpoví.“
listen	what	(he) answers

Večer	se	zvedl	vítr	a	do	místnosti
(In the) evening	itself	picked up	(the) wind	and	into	(the) room

vletělo	Slunce,	starý	děda	se	zlatou
flew in	(the) sun	(the) old	grandfather	himself	(with the) golden

hlavou.
head

„Čuchám	člověčinu!“	zvolal.	„Někoho	tu
(I) smell	(a) human being	(he) exclaimed	Someone	here

máš,	matko?“
(you) have	mother

„Ale	prosím	tě,“	řekla	babička,	„koho	bych
But	please	you	said	(the) old woman	whom	(I) would

tu měla? To ty se celý den touláš
here had This you yourself (the) whole day (you) wander

po světě, a pak ti všude voní člověk."
through (the) world and then you everywhere smells man

Děd Vševěd nic neřekl a sedl si
Grandfather Vsheved All-knowing nothing said and sat down himself

k večeři.
to dinner

Po večeři položil babičce svou zlatou
After dinner (he) placed (to the) old woman his golden

hlavu na klín a usnul. Když babička
head on (her) lap and fell asleep When (the) old woman

viděla, že už spí, vytrhla mu jeden
saw that already (he) sleeps (she) ripped off him one

zlatý vlas a hodila na zem – zazvonil jako
golden hair and tossed on (the) ground – (it) rang like

struna. „Co chceš, matko?" řekl stařeček.
(a) string What (you) want mother said (the) old man

„Nic, synáčku, nic! dřímala jsem jen a měla
Nothing son nothing snoozing (I) am only and had

jsem divný sen.“ –
(I) am (a) weird dream –

„A co se ti zdálo?“ –
And what yourself you (it) seemed –
dreamed

„Zdálo se mi o jednom městě, měli tam
(It) seemed itself me about one city had there
I dreamed

pramen živé vody: když byl někdo nemocný
(a) source (with) living water when was someone sick
a spring

a napil se jí, uzdravil se; a když
and (he) drank himself her healed by himself and when

umřel a tou vodou ho pokropili, znovu ožil.
(he) died and that water him sprinkled again (he) revived

Ale už dvacet let voda tam ta voda
But already twenty years (the) water there this water

neteče: dá se něco udělat, aby
does not flow can oneself something do in order that

znovu proudila?“ –
again (she) flows –

„Jednoduše: v té studně na prameni sedí žába,
Simple in that well in (the) spring sits (a) frog

kvůli ní voda neteče; ať žábu zabíjí
due to (of) her (the) water does not flow let that (the) frog kills
is killed

a studnici vyčistí, pak bude voda znovu
and (the) well clears then will (the) water again

proudit.“ –
stream –

Když stařeček potom znovu usnul, vytrhla mu
When (the) old man then again fell asleep ripped off him

babička druhý zlatý vlas a hodila ho na
(the) old woman (an) other golden hair and tossed it on

zem. „Což zase máš, matko?“
(the) ground Which again (you) have mother

„Nic, synáčku, nic! Dřímala jsem a
Nothing son nothing Snoozing (I) am and

zdálo	se	mi	opět	něco	divného.
(it) seemed	itself	(to) me	again	something	weird
	I dreamed				

Zdálo	se	mí	o	jednom	městě,	měli	tam
(It) seemed	itself	me	about	one	city	had	there
	I dreamed					where was	

jabloň,	plodila	jablka	mládí:	když	někdo
(an) apple tree	spawned by	apples	(of) youth	when	someone

zestárnul	a	jedno	snědl,	opět	omládl.	Ale
aged	and	one	ate	again	(he) rejuvenated	But

už	dvacet	let	jabloň	neplodí	ovoce:
already	twenty	years	(the) apple tree	not procreates	fruit

jak	to	napravit?“	–
how	this	to fix?	–

„Jednoduše:	pod	jabloní	leží	had,	užírá	jí
Simple	under	(the) apple tree	lies	(a) snake	takes	her

síly:	ať	hada	zabijí	a	jabloň	přesadí,
forces	let that	(the) snake	kills	and	(the) apple tree	relocate

bude	dávat	zas	ovoce	jako	kdysi.“	–
will	give	again	fruit	as	once upon a time	–

Potom	stařeček	brzy	opět	usnul	a
Then	(the) old man	soon	again	fell asleep	and

babička	mu	vytrhla	třetí	zlatý	vlas:
(the) old woman	him	ripped off	(the) third	golden	hair

„Nenecháš	mě,	matko,	spát?“	řekl	stařeček
(You) won't let	me	mother	(to) sleep	said	(the) old man

mrzutě	a	chtěl	už	vstávat.
grimly	and	wanted	already	to get up

„Lež,	synáčku,	lež!	Nehněvej	se,	nerada
Lie	son	lie	Don't be angry	yourself	(I) don't like

jsem	tě	vzbudila.	Ale	přišla	na	mě	dřímota	a
(I) am	you	aroused	However	came	to	me	slumber	and

měla	jsem	zas	podivný	sen.	Zdálo	se	mi	o
had	(I) am	again	(a) weird	dream	(It) seemed	itself	me	about
					I dreamed			

přívozníkovi	na	černém	moři:	dvacet	let	už
(a) ferryman	on	(the) black	sea	twenty	years	already

tam	převáží	a	nikdo	ho	nedokáže
there	(he is) transports	and	no one	him	can't

vysvobodit. Kdy bude svobodný od své práce?“
deliver / set free — When — (he) will be — free — from — his — work

–
–

„Hloupé matky to syn! ať dá jinému
Stupid — mother — this — son (has) — let that — (he) gives — to another

veslo do ruky a sám vyskočí na břeh,
(the) oar — into — (the) hand — and — himself — will pop up — on — (the) shore

bude ten zas přívozníkem. Ale teď už
will be — that one / the other person — again — (be) ferryman — But — now — already

mi dej pokoj: musím časně ráno vstát a jít
me — give — rest — (I) have to — early — morning — get up — and — go

sušit slzy, které králova dcera každou noc
dry — (the) tears — which — (the) king's — daughter — each — night

vypláče pro svého muže, uhlířova syna,
cries — for — her — husband — (the) charcoal maker's — son

kterého král poslal pro mé tři zlaté vlasy.“
who — (the) king — sent — for — my — three — (a) golden — hairs

K ránu strhl se znovu venku vítr
At (the) morning pulled down itself again outside (the) wind
calmed down

a na klíně své staré matičky probudilo se,
and on (the) lap (of) his old little mother woke up himself

místo stařečka, krásné zlatovlasé dítě,
(in the) place (of the) old man (a) beautiful (with) goldilocks child

boží Sluněčko, rozloučilo se se svou
(the) divine Sunshine (he) said goodbye himself from his

starou matičkou a východním oknem vyletělo
old mother and (through the) eastern window out-flew

ven. Babička zas odklopila káď a řekla
out (The) old woman again unplugged (the) vat and (she) said
lifted the lid of the vat

Plaváčkovi: „Tady máš zlaté vlasy, a co
(to) Floater Here (you) have (the) golden hairs and what

Děd Vševěd na ty tři věci odpověděl,
Grandfather All-knowing on those three things answered

už taky víš. Dobře dojdi! Už mě víc
already also know Good go to Already me more

neuhlídáš,	není	to	třeba.“	Plaváček
(you) can't watch	not is	this	possible	Floater

babičce	pěkně	poděkoval	a	šel.
(to the) old woman	nicely politely	thanked	and	(he) went

Když	přišel	do	toho	prvního	města,	ptal	se
When	(he) came	to	this	first	city	asked	himself

ho	král,	jakou	jim	nese	novinu?	–	„Dobrou!“
him	(the) king	which	them	carried	news	–	Good

řekl	Plaváček,	„dejte	studnu	vyčistit	a	žábu,	co
said	Floater	let (you)	(the) well	clean out	and	(a) frog	that

na	prameně	sedí,	zabijte	a	poteče	vám	voda	zas
in	(the) source	sits	kill	and	will flow	your	water	again

jako	kdysi.“	–
like	once upon a time	–

Král	to	nechal	hned	udělat,	a	když	viděl,	že
(The) king	this	let	now	do	and	when	(he) saw	that

se	voda	řítí	plným	pramenem,	daroval
itself	(the) water	rushing	full	(from the) source	(he) gifted

Plaváčkovi dvanáct koní bílých jako labutě a k
(to) Floater twelve horses white like swans and to

nim tolik zlata a stříbra a drahého kamení,
them so much gold and silver and expensive stones

co mohli unést.
as (they) could carry away

Když přišel do toho druhého města, ptal se
When (he) came to this other second city asked himself

ho zase král, jakou jim nese novinu? –
him again (the) king which them carried news –

„Dobrou!“ řekl Plaváček, „dejte jabloň vykopat,
Good said Floater let (the) apple tree dig up

najdete pod kořeny hada, toho zabijte; potom
(you) find under (the) roots (a) snake this kill then

jabloň znovu zasaďte a ponese vám ovoce
(the) apple tree again plant and (it) will carry your fruit

jako kdysi.“ –
like once upon a time –

Král	to	dal	hned	udělat,	a	jabloň
(The) king	this	gave	now	to do	and	(the) apple tree

byla	za	noc	posetá	květy,	jakoby	ji
(she) was	after	(a) night	dotted	(with) flowers	as if	her

růžemi	osypal.	Král	měl	velikou	radost	a
roses	sprinkled	(The) king	had	great	joy	and

daroval	Plaváčkovi	dvanáct	koní	vraných	jako
gifted	(to) Floater	twelve	horses	raven-colored black	like

havrani,	a	na	ně	taky	tolik	bohatství,	co
ravens	and	on	them	so	much	wealth	what

mohli	unést.
(they) could	carry away

Plaváček	jel	potom	dál,	a	když	byl	u
Floater	(he) rode	then	further	and	when	(he) was	at

černého	moře,	ptal	se	ho	přívozník,	jestli
(the) black	sea	asked	himself	him	(the) ferryman	if

se	dověděl,	kdy	bude	vysvobozen?
himself	(he) found out	when	(he) will be	delivered

„Dověděl," řekl Plaváček, „ale nejdřív mě převez,
(I) found out said Floater but first me transport

pak ti to povím." – Přívozník se sice
then you this (I) will tell – (The) ferryman himself although

vzpouzel, ale když viděl, že jinak to nepůjde,
rebelled but when (he) saw that otherwise this won't work

převezl ho i s jeho čtyřmi a dvaceti
(he) transported him and with his four and twenty

koňmi. „Až zas budeš někoho převážet," řekl mu
horses When again (you) will someone transport said him

potom Plaváček, „dej mu veslo do ruky a
then Floater give him (the) oar to (the) hand and

vyskoč na břeh, a bude ten místo tebe
pop up on shore and will this one (in) place (of) you

přívozníkem,"
(be the) ferryman

Král ani nevěřil svým očím, když mu
(The) king (his father-in-law) neither disbelieved his eyes when him

Plaváček ty tři zlaté vlasy Děda Vševěda
Floater those three golden hairs (of) Grandfather Vsheved
All-knowing

přinesl, a jeho dcera plakala, ne smutkem, ale
brought and his daughter cried not (with) sadness but

radostí, že se zas vrátil. „A kde jsi
joy that himself again (he) returned And where (you) are

získal ty pěkné koně a to veliké
retrieved from you nice horses and this great

bohatství?“ ptal se král.
wealth asked himself (the) king

„Vysloužil jsem si ho,“ řekl Plaváček a
Earned (I) am myself it said Floater and

vypravoval, jak tomu králi pomohl k jablkům,
narrated how this king (he) helped to apples

které ze starých lidí dělají mladé, a tomu
which from old people made young and that

králi k živé vodě, která z nemocných dělá
king to living water which from (the) sick makes

zdravé a z mrtvých živé, – „Jablka mládí!
(the) healthy and from (the) dead alive – Apples (of) youth!

Živá voda!“ opakoval si potichu král,
Living water! repeated himself quietly (the) king

„kdybych jedno snědl, omládl bych, a kdybych
if would one (I) ate rejuvenated (I) would and if would

i zemřel, tou vodou bych zas ožil!“ Bez
also (I) died that water (I) would again revived Without

meškání vydal se na cestu pro jablka
delays gave out directed himself on (a) journey for (the) apples

mládí a pro živou vodu – a dosud se
(of) youth and for (the) living water – and so far himself

ještě nevrátil.
(he) still not returned

A tak se stal uhlířův syn
And so himself became (the) charcoal burner's son

zetěm královým, jak Sudička usoudila, a
(the) son-in-law (of the) king like (the) Judge the weird sister concluded and

král	–	snad	doteď	tam	pořád	převáží	přes
(the) king	–	perhaps	so far until now	there	still	carried over transports	over

černé	moře!
(the) black	sea!

Zlatovláska
Goldenhairs

Byl	jednou	jeden	král,	který	rozuměl
(There) was	once	a	king	who	understood

řeči	všech	zvířat.	A	jak	se	to	naučil?
(the) speech	(of) all	animals	And	how	himself	this	(he) learned

Jednoho	dne	přišla	k	němu	stará	babička	s
One	day	came	to	him	old	old woman	with
					an old	woman	

košíkem.	Měla	v	něm	hada.	Řekla	králi:
(a) basket	(She) had	in	it	(a) snake	(She) told	(the) king

„Nechte	si	tohoto	hada	připravit	k	obědu.
Let	yourself	this	snake	prepare	for	lunch

Když	ho	sníte,	porozumíte	všemu,	co
When	it	(you) eat	(you) will understand	to all	what

říkají	zvířata	v	oblacích,	na	zemi	i	ve
(they) say	(the) animals	in	(the) clouds	on	(the) country	and	in

vodě.“
(the) water

Králi se ta nabídka zalíbila, dobře
(The) king himself this offer liked good

babičce zaplatil a poručil svému
(to the) old woman paid and commanded his

sloužícímu Jiříkovi, aby hada připravil.
servant Jirik in order that (the) snake (he) prepared

„Ale pamatuj,“ dodal, „ani kousek neochutnej,
But remember (he) added not even (a) piece not taste

jinak za to zaplatíš svou hlavou!“
otherwise for this (you) pay your head

Jiřík byl zvědavý. „Had k obědu?“ říkal si.
Jirik was curious Snake for lunch (he) told himself

„To jsem ještě neviděl. Ale jaký by to byl
This (I) am still not saw But how would this was
I have never seen be

kuchař, kdyby neochutnal, co připravuje?“ Když
(a) chef if (he) not tasted what preparing When
he prepares

byl had upečený, vzal Jiřík kousek na jazyk.
was (the) snake baked took Jirik (a) piece on (the) tongue

V tom uslyšel slabé hlasy: „Dej nám také
In that (he) heard weak voices Give us also
At that moment

něco! Dej nám také něco!“ Rozhlédl
something Give us also something (He) looked around

se a viděl mouchy létající kolem. Pak venku
himself and (he) saw flies flying around Then outside

uslyšel: „Kam jdeš? Kam jdeš?“ A jemnější hlasy
(he) heard Where (you) go Where (you) go And finer voices

odpovídaly: „Do mlynářova ječmene, do mlynářova
answered To (the) miller's barley to (the) miller's

ječmene.“ Jiřík vykoukl z okna a uviděl
barley Jirik peeked from (the) window and (he) saw

housera s hejnem hus.
(a) gander with (a) flock (of) geese

„Aha!“ řekl si, „tohle ten had umí!“
Aha (he) said (to) himself this -the- snake can
enabled (me to)

Dal	si	ještě	jeden	malý	kousek	a	pak
(He) gave	himself	still	one	small	piece	and	then

zbytek	přinesl	králi.
(the) rest	brought	(to the) king

Po	obědě	král	nařídil	Jiříkovi,	aby
After	lunch	(the) king	ordered	Jirik	in order that

osedlal	koně,	že	se	chtějí	projet.
(he) saddled	(the) horses	that	themselves	(they) want	to ride out

Král	jel	vepředu,	Jiřík	za	ním.
(The) king	rode	in front	Jirik	behind	him

Když	projížděli	zelenou	loukou,	Jiříkův
When	(they) drove through	(a) green	meadow	Jirik's
	they were driving through			

kůň	zařehtal:	„Bratře,	mně	je	tak	lehko,	že
horse	neighed	Brother	to me	(it) is	so	light	that

bych	přes	hory	skákal!“
(I) would	over	(the) mountain	jumped
I could			jump

Druhý	kůň	odpověděl:	„Já	bych	také	rád,	ale	na
(The) other	horse	answered	I	would	also	gladly	but	on

mně	sedí	starý.	Kdybych	skočil,	spadl	by
to me	sits	(the) old (guy)	If (I) would	jumped	dropped	would
				jump	he would fall	

a	zlomil	si	vaz.“
and	broke	himself	(the) neck

„Ať	si	ho	zlomí!“	řekl	první.	„Pak	budeš
Let	himself	it	break	said	first	Then	(you) will
					the first one		

nosit	mladého!“
carry	(a) young (one)

Jiřík	se	rozesmál,	ale	jen	tiše.	Král	se
Jirik	-himself-	laughed	but	only	quietly	(The) king	himself

však	otočil	a	zeptal	se:	„Čemu
however	turned around	and	asked	-himself-	Why

se	směješ?“
-yourself-	laugh
	do you laugh

„Jen	tak,	něco	mi	přišlo	na	mysl,“	odpověděl
Only	so	something	me	arrived	on	(the) mind	answered

Jiřík.	Král	už	ale	Jiříkovi	nevěřil.
Jirik	(The) king	already	but	Jirik	disbelieved
		however			did not believe

Když se vrátili do zámku, král řekl:
When themselves (they) returned to (the) castle (the) king said

„Jiříku, nalej mi víno, ale pozor! Jestli
Jirik pour me wine but attention If

přelejecomplex nebo nedoleješ, zaplatíš za to
(you) pour over or don't pour enough (you) pay for this
you pour too much

hlavou!“
(with the) head

Jiřík vzal konvici a začal lít.
Jirik took (the) jug and started to pour

Najednou přiletěli dva ptáčci. Jeden nesl v
At once arrived two birds One carried in

zobáku tři zlaté vlasy a druhý na něj křičel:
(the) beak three golden hairs and (the) other at him shouted

„Dej mi je! Jsou moje!“
Give me them (They) are mine

„Ne, jsou moje! Já je našel!“
No (they) are mine I them found

„Ale já je viděl dřív, když je ztratila
But I them saw sooner when them lost
first

Zlatovláska při česání!“
Goldilocks at combing

Prali se o vlasy a nakonec každý
(They) fought each other over (the) hairs and finally each

dostal jeden, ale třetí zlatý vlas upadl Jiříkovi
acquired one but (the) third golden hair dropped Jirik

k noham. Když se po něm Jiřík ohlédl,
to (the) feet When himself on it Jirik looked back

přelil víno.
overpoured (the) wine

„Neposlechl jsi můj příkaz!“ vykřikl král.
Disobeyed (you) are my command exclaimed (the) king
you have

„Ale dám ti šanci na milost. Přiveď mi
But (I) will give you (a) chance on grace Bring me
one chance to get

Zlatovlásku za ženu!“
Goldilocks for woman
as wife

Co měl Jiřík dělat? Musel vyrazit na cestu, i
What had Jirik to do (He) must go out on (the) road and

když nevěděl, kde Zlatovlásku najít.
while (he) didn't know where Goldilocks to find

—
—

Jel dlouho a přišel k černému lesu. Uviděl,
(He) rode long and came to (the) black forest (He) saw

jak na kraji lesa hoří keř, který
how on (the) edge (of the) forest burns (a) bush which

zapálili pasáci. Pod keřem byl mraveniště
set on fire (the) herders Under (the) bush was (an) anthill
was set on fire by

a mravenci zoufale volali: „Pomoz, Jiříku! Shoříme
and (the) ants desperate called Help Jirik We'll burn

i s našimi vajíčky!“
and with our eggs
also

Jiřík seskočil z koně, uhasil oheň a
Jirik jumped off from (his) horse put out (the) fire and

zachránil mravence. „Děkujeme ti! Až nás budeš
saved (the) ants Thank you When us (you) will

potřebovat, pomůžeme ti!“ volali mravenci.
need (we) can help you called (the) ants

Jiřík pokračoval lesem, až přišel k vysoké
Jirik continued (through the) forest then came to (a) high

jedli. Na zemi pod stromem naříkala dvě
fir tree On (the) ground under (the) tree lamented two

malá krkavčata: „Rodiče nám uletěli a my
small ravens Parents ours (they) flew away and we

sami potravu najít neumíme. Umřeme hlady!“
ourselves food find (we) can't (We will) die hungrily

Jiřík se nerozmýšlel, zabil svého koně, aby
Jirik himself not thinking killed his horse in order that

měli co jíst. Krkavčata radostně krákorala:
(they) had what something to eat (The) ravens joyfully crowed

„Děkujeme ti! Až nás budeš potřebovat,
Thank you When us (you) will need

pomůžeme ti!“
(we) can help you

Bez koně šel Jiřík dál pěšky. Došel až
Without horses went Jirik further on foot (He) reached then

k moři, kde uviděl dva rybáře hádat se
to (the) sea where (he) saw two fishermen quarrel themselves
with each other

o velkou zlatou rybu. „Je moje!“ křičel jeden.
over (a) great golden fish (She) is mine shouted one

„Ne, moje!“ křičel druhý. Jiřík je uklidnil:
No mine shouted (the) other Jirik them calmed down

„Prodejte mi ji a peníze si rozdělíte!“
Sell me her and (the) money yourselves split

Rybáři souhlasili. Jiřík pustil zlatou rybu
(The) fisherman agreed Jirik let (the) golden fish

zpět do moře. Ta vystrčila hlavu z
back into (the) sea That one pushed out (the) head from

vody a řekla: „Děkuji ti! Až mě budeš
(the) water and said Thank you Then me (you) will

potřebovat, pomůžu ti!“
need I'll help you

„Kam jdeš?“ zeptali se ho rybáři. Jiřík
Where (you) go asked -themselves- him (the) fisherman Jirik

jim vyprávěl o Zlatovlásce. „To je dcera
them (he) told about Goldilocks That is (the) daughter

krále z Křišťálového zámku na ostrově,“
(of the) king from (the) Crystal castle on (the) island

řekli mu. „Každé ráno si češá své
(they) said to him Each morning herself (she) combs her

zlaté vlasy, a jejich záře osvětluje moře i
golden hairs and their glow illuminates (the) sea and

nebe. Dovezeme tě tam.“
(the) sky (We will) deliver you there

Rybáři naložili Jiříka na loď a
(The) fisherman embarked Jirik on (a) boat and

odvezli ho na ostrov. Ale varovali ho:
(they) took away him to (the) island But (they) warned him

„Dávej si pozor. Zlatovlásek je dvanáct, ale
Give yourself attention Goldilocks is twelve but
Pay - There are twelve Goldilocks

jen jedna má zlaté vlasy!“
only one has golden hairs

Když Jiřík dorazil na ostrov, šel rovnou do
When Jirik arrived on (the) island (he) went straight to

Křišťálového zámku. Prosil krále, aby
(the) Crystal castle (He) asked (the) king in order that

dal svou Zlatovlásku za manželku jeho pánovi,
(he) gave his Goldilocks for wife (to) his lord

starému králi.
to the old king

Král řekl: „Dám ti ji, ale musíš si ji
(The) king said (I) will give you her but (you) must yourself her

zasloužit. Budeš mít tři úkoly, jeden na každý
earn (You) will have three tasks one on each

den. Pokud je splníš, Zlatovláska bude tvého
day If them (you) will fulfill Goldilocks will be of your

pána. Dnes si odpočiň a zítra začneš."
lord Today yourself relax and tomorrow (you) will start

—
—

Druhý den ráno král řekl: „Zlatovlásce
(The) other day (in the) morning (the) king said Goldilocks
The next

se přetrhla šňůrka perel a perly se
herself broke (a) string (of) pearls and (the) pearls themselves

rozsypaly po zelené louce. Ty je musíš
spilled on (the) green meadow You them must

všechny najít. Ani jedna nesmí chybět."
all find Neither one must not miss
Not even

Jiřík šel na louku. Byla obrovská a rostla na
Jirik (he) went on meadow (It) was huge and grew on

ní vysoká tráva. Klekl si a začal hledat,
her tall grass (He) kneeled himself and started to search

ale nenašel jedinou perlu. Hledal celé dopoledne
but not found (a) single pearl Searched (a) full morning

a už byl zoufalý. „Kdyby tu byli moji
and already was desperate If here were my

mravenci, ti by mi pomohli!“ vzdychl.
ants those would me helped (he) sighed

V tom uslyšel tenké hlásky: „Jsme tady,
In this (he) heard thin sounds (We) are here
At that moment

abychom ti pomohli!“ Najednou se kolem
in order that to you (we) helped At once themselves around

Jiříka začalo hemžit spoustu mravenců. „Co
Jirik started to swarm lots of ants What

potřebuješ?“ ptali se. Jiřík řekl, že
(you) need (they) asked -themselves- Jirik said that

musí najít všechny perly v trávě. „Počkej
(he) must find all pearls in (the) grass Wait

chvíli, my je najdeme za tebe,“ řekli mravenci.
(a) while we them (will) find for you said (the) ants

Za chvíli snesli na hromádku všechny
After (a) while (they) carried on (a) pile all

perly.	Jiřík	je	navlékl	na	tkanici,	a	když
(the) pearls	Jirik	them	put on	on	(a) lace	and	when

už	chtěl	zavázat	uzel,	přiběhl	chromý
already	wanted	to tie	(a) knot	ran up	(a) lame

mravenec.	„Počkej,	Jiříku!“	volal.	„Nesu	ještě
ant	Wait	Jirik	(he) called	(I) carry	still

jednu	perlu!“	Byla	to	poslední,	která	chyběla.
one	pearl	Was	this	(the) last one	which	missed
		That one was				

Jiřík	přinesl	šňůrku	perel	králi.	Ten	je
Jirik	brought	(the) string	(of) pearls	(to the) king	This one	them

přepočítal	a	spokojeně	řekl:	„Dobrá	práce!
recounted	and	satisfied	said	Good	work

Zítra	dostaneš	další	úkol.“
Tomorrow	you'll get	(a) further	task
		another	

—

—

Druhý	den	ráno	král	řekl:	„Zlatovlásce
(The) other	day	(in the) morning	(the) king	said	Goldilocks
The next					

spadl do moře zlatý prsten. Najdi ho a
dropped into (the) sea (a) golden ring Find it and

přines ho zpět."
bring it back

Jiřík šel k moři. Chodil po břehu a díval
Jirik (he) went to sea (He) walked on (the) shore and looked

se na hladinu. Moře bylo průzračné, ale
himself at (the water) surface (The) sea was transparent but

tak hluboké, že neviděl na dno. „Kdyby tu
so deep that (he) not saw to (the) bottom If here

byla má zlatá ryba, ta by mi pomohla!"
was my golden fish this one would me helped

povzdechl si.
(he) sighed himself

Najednou se voda rozčeřila a zlatá ryba
At once itself (the) water stirred and (the) golden fish

vyplula na hladinu. „Jsem tady, abych ti
swam on (the) surface (I) am here so that you

pomohla,“ řekla. „Co potřebuješ?“
(I) helped (she) said What (you) need

Jiřík jí vysvětlil, že hledá zlatý prsten
Jirik her explained that (he was) looking for (a) golden ring

na dně moře. „Zrovna jsem potkala
on (the) bottom (of the) sea Just (I) am stumbled upon
Only just

štiku, co měla prsten na ploutvi. Počkej chvíli,
(a) pike what had (a) ring on (the) fins Wait (a) while
who

přinesu ti ho.“
I'll bring you it

Za chvíli se ryba vrátila a přinesla
After (a) while herself (the) fish returned and brought along

Jiříkovi prsten. Jiřík poděkoval a hned běžel za
Jirik's ring Jirik thanked (her) and now ran for

králem. Král si prsten prohlédl a řekl:
(the) king (The) king himself (the) ring viewed and said

„Dobrá práce! Třetí úkol bude ten nejtěžší.“
Good work (The) third task will be this one (the) hardest

—

—

Třetí den ráno král řekl: „Chceš-li,
(The) third day (in the) morning (the) king said If you want

abych dal Zlatovlásku tvému pánovi, musíš
so that (I) gave Goldilocks to your lord (you) must

přinést mrtvou a živou vodu. Budeme ji
fetch dead and living water (We) will her

potřebovat.“
need

Jiřík nevěděl, kde takovou vodu hledat. Šel
Jirik didn't know where such water to search (He) went

lesem, až si povzdechl: „Kdyby tu
(through the) forest then himself sighed If here

byli moji krkavci, snad by mi pomohli!“ Náhle
were my ravens perhaps would me (they) helped Suddenly

uslyšel nad sebou šustění. Dva krkavci přiletěli a
(he) heard over himself rustling Two ravens arrived and

řekli: „Jsme tady, abychom ti pomohli. Co
(they) said (We) are here so that you (we) helped What

potřebuješ?“
(do you) need

Jiřík jim pověděl o mrtvé a živé vodě.
Jirik them told about (the) dead and living water

Krkavci odpověděli: „O té vodě víme. Počkej
(The) ravens answered About that water (we) know Wait

chvíli, přineseme ti ji.“ Za chvíli se
(a) while (we'll) bring you her After (a) while themselves

vrátili. Každý nesl jednu tykvici: v jedné byla
(they) returned Each carried one gourd in one was

mrtvá voda, ve druhé živá.
dead water in (the) other living

Cestou zpět Jiřík viděl mezi stromy obrovskou
(On the) way back Jirik saw between (the) trees (a) huge

pavučinu. V ní seděl velký pavouk a cucal
spider web In (of) her sat (a) large spider and sucked

mouchu.	Jiřík	vzal	mrtvou	vodu	a	postříkal
fly	Jirik	took	dead	water	and	splashed

pavouka.	Pavouk	spadl	mrtvý	na	zem.
(the) spider	(The) spider	dropped	dead	on	(the) ground

Potom	vzal	živou	vodu	a	pokropil	mouchu.
Then	(he) took	living	water	and	sprinkled	(the) fly

Moucha	se	probudila,	zamávala	křídly	a
(The) fly	himself	woke up	waved	(the) wings	and
			fluttered		

řekla:	„Děkuji,	Jiříku!	Zachránil	jsi	mi	život.	Já
said	Thank (you)	Jirik	Saved	(you) are	my	life	I
				you have			

ti	teď	pomůžu.	Až	budeš	vybírat	Zlatovlásku
you	now	(will) help	When	(you) will	choose	Goldilocks

mezi	dvanácti	pannami,	povím	ti,	která	z	nich
between	twelve	virgins	(I'll) tell	you	who	from	them

to	je.“
this	is

—

—

Když Jiřík přinesl vodu, král řekl: „Správně
When Jirik brought water (the) king said Right
Correctly

jsi splnil všechny úkoly. Teď si můžeš
(you) are met all tasks Now yourself (you) can
you have fulfilled

Zlatovlásku vzít, ale musíš ji poznat. Přivedu
Goldilocks take but must her recognize (I will) bring

dvanáct dívek. Jen jedna z nich je Zlatovláska.“
twelve girls Only one from them is Goldilocks

Král zavedl Jiříka do velké síně. U kulatého
(The) king escorted Jirik into (a) great hall At (a) round

stolu sedělo dvanáct krásných dívek. Každá měla
table sat twelve beautiful girls Each had

na hlavě bílý závoj, takže nebylo vidět jejich
on (the) head (a) white veil so not was to see their

vlasy.
hairs

Jiřík nevěděl, co dělat. V tom mu něco
Jirik didn't know what to do In this him something
At this moment

zašeptalo do ucha: „Bz, bz! Já ti pomůžu. Pojď,
whispered into (the) ear Bz bz I you (will) help Go

řeknu ti, která je ta pravá." Byla to moucha,
(I) say (to) you who is this right (one) Was this (the) fly

kterou zachránil. Letěla kolem dívek a šeptala:
who (he) saved (She) flew around (the) girls and whispered

„Tahle ne, tahle taky ne... Támhle ta je
This one no this one also no Over there this is

Zlatovláska!"
Goldilocks

Jiřík ukázal na dívku. „Tuto mi dej!" řekl.
Jirik pointed at (the) girl This (one) me give (he) said

Dívka vstala, sundala závoj, a její zlaté vlasy
(The) girl got up took down (the) veil and her golden hairs

zazářily jako slunce. Jiříkovi se z toho lesku
shone like (the) sun Jirik himself from this shine

až zatočila hlava.
then turned (the) head

Král souhlasil a bohatě obstaral princeznu na
(The) king agreed and richly procured (the) princess on

cestu. Jiřík odvezl Zlatovlásku ke svému pánovi,
(the) road Jirik led out Goldilocks to his lord

starému králi. Starému králi se jiskřily oči
(to the) old (the) king (The) old king himself sparkled (the) eyes

a poskakoval radostí, když Zlatovlásku uviděl, a
and bounced (with) joy when Goldilocks (he) saw and

hned rozkázal, aby se začala připravovat
now commanded in order that himself started to prepare

jeho svatba.
his wedding

„Chtěl jsem tě sice dát oběsit pro tvou
Wanted (I) am you although (you) give to hang for your
you let hang

neposlušnost, aby tě snědli krkavci," povídá
disobedience in order that you ate (the) ravens (he) told

Jiříkovi, „ale protože mi tak dobře posloužil,
Jirik but because me so good (you) served

dám	ti	jen	srazit	hlavu	sekyrou,	a	pak
(I) will give	you	only	to cut off	(the) head	(with an) axe	and	then
I will let			cut off				

tě	dám	počestně	pochovat.“
you	(I) will give	(an) honest	burial

Když	Jiříka	popravili,	prosila	Zlatovláska	starého
When	Jirik	(they) executed	begged	Goldilocks	(the) old

krále,	aby	jí	toho	mrtvého	služebníka
king	in order that	her	this	dead	servant

daroval,	a	král	nemohl	své	zlatovlasé	nevěstě
(he) gifted	and	(the) king	couldn't	his	golden-haired	bride

její	přání	nijak	odepřít.	Potom	srovnala	hlavu
her	wishes	nothing	to deny	Then	(she) compared	(the) head
					she put on	

Jiříkovu	k	jeho	tělu,	pokropila	ho	mrtvou	vodou,
(of) Jirik	to	his	body	sprinkled	him	(with) dead	water

a	tělo	srostlo	s	hlavou,	takže	po	ráně
and	(the) body	grew	with	(the) head	so	on	(the) wound

nezbyla	ani	památka.	Pak	ho	pokropila	živou
not left	neither	memory	Then	him	sprinkled	(with) live
	not even					

vodou, a Jiřík vstal, jakoby se byl znovu
water and Jirik stood up as if himself was again

narodil, hbitý jako jelen a mladost mu svítila
born agile like (a) deer and youth him shone

z tváří.
from (the) face

„Och, to jsem ale tvrdě spal!“ povídá Jiřík a
Oh this (I) am but hard slept says Jirik and
I have indeed deeply

mnul si oči. „Opravdu, tvrdě jsi spal,“
rubbed himself (the) eyes Really hard (you) are slept
you have

řekla Zlatovláska, „a kdyby nebylo mě, na věky
said Goldilocks and if not was me on ages

věků bys ses neprobudil!“ –
of the ages (you) would (you) are yourself not woken up –
(se + s)

Když starý král viděl, žc Jiřík zase ožil, a že
When (the) old king saw that Jirik again revived and that

je mladší a krásnější než předtím, toužil
(he) is younger and more beautiful than before (he) desired

také takto omládnout. Hned poručil, aby
also like so to get younger Now (he) commanded in order that

mu sťali hlavu a pak pokropili tou
him (they) cut off (the) head and then sprinkled (with) that

kouzelnou vodou.
magic water

Sťali mu tedy hlavu a kropili živou
(They) beheaded him so (the) head and sprinkled live

vodou pořád, pořád, až ji všechnu vykropili: ale
water still still then her all of them they robbed but

hlava nijak mu nechtěla k tělu přirůst;
(the) head nothing him didn't want to (the) body grow

potom teprve začali kropit mrtvou vodou,
then only (they) started to sprinkle dead water

a rázem srostla: ale král byl opět mrtev,
and at once grew but (the) king was again dead

protože už neměli živou vodu, aby ho
because already (they) not had live water in order that him

vzkřísili.
(they) resurrected

A poněvadž království bez krále nemohlo
And whereas (the) kingdom without (a) king couldn't

fungovat, a nebyl nikdo tak rozumný, kdo
function and (there) was not no one so reasonable smart who

by rozuměl všem živočichům jako Jiřík, udělali
would understood to all animals like Jirik (they) made

z Jiříka krále a ze Zlatovlásky královnu.
from Jirik (the) king and from Goldilocks (the) queen

www.ingramcontent.com/pod-product-compliance
Lightning Source LLC
Chambersburg PA
CBHW071331250626
47159CB00004B/1563

* 9 7 8 1 8 3 4 2 5 1 0 8 0 *